Tony Jenkins was born in South Wales and first worked in the coal mines as a mining surveyor, before joining the RAF for training as a navigator. After completing his service, he had no wish to return to coal mining and joined an international company to work in sales and marketing. Following appointments in sales management, training and general management, he was appointed managing director of a subsidiary company. With a wide range of experience, he then decided to become self employed as a management consultant before retiring to travel, play tennis and begin writing.

My first book in the *Seniors* series is dedicated to my wife, Margaret, who found scribbled notes for novels I was always going to write and convinced me that I should give up building walls and get writing. Her help in spotting errors or spelling mistakes, as a meticulous proof-reader, was invaluable, as also was the support and encouragement of our large family and friends.

Tony Jenkins

Senior Singles

Austin Macauley Publishers™
London • Cambridge • New York • Sharjah

A CIP catalogue record for this title is available from the British Library.

ISBN 9781398406322 (Paperback)
ISBN 9781398406339 (Hardback)
ISBN 9781398402324 (ePub e-book)
ISBN 9781398406346 (Audiobook)

www.austinmacauley.com

First Published (2021)
Austin Macauley Publishers Ltd
25 Canada Square
Canary Wharf
London
E14 5LQ

Once the euphoria of having a manuscript accepted for publishing is over, for the author, the long process of involvement in converting it into a published book begins. Austin Macauley provides encouragement and guidance at each stage, which not only shapes the book, but also helps to improve the writing skills of the author.

Chapter 1
Acceptance

Standing with family and friends in the small chapel, the preacher spoke about the wonderful woman who had been my wife. After meeting as teenagers, we became engaged two years later and together produced three great children and moved to bigger houses and new locations as my career progressed. We sang the last hymn and then the coffin carrying my wife began to glide quietly away, and when it disappeared behind the curtain shield, the tears trickled down my cheeks. My clever, patient, loving Mary was now gone forever.

The children gathered around me and we hugged, but we were all so full of emotion that speech was impossible. My name is Tom Hartley and I had just lost my wife after thirty-five years of very happy marriage, leaving me a widower and my children without a mother. I have two daughters, Karen, who is married, and Abby, who has just left university to start a career in sales promotion. My son, Michael, works in Australia but returned for his mother's funeral. After the service, we returned to the family house where my daughters had arranged food and drinks. We had a wide circle of friends through my business contacts and involvement in the local golf and tennis clubs. The house was filled with people offering sympathy and support, but without Mary to supervise the catering and stand beside me to greet visitors, I suddenly felt very much alone. The dishes were washed and put away and after all the goodbyes had been said; family and friends returned to their homes and left me alone in a big, empty, echoing house. Michael had to return to his work and was already on his way back to Australia.

After being half of a loving active couple for over thirty years, it was difficult to accept being a widower. Having recently retired, there were no work colleagues or demanding customers to take up my time and patience. The house was once filled with the noise of children banging doors and stomping up and down stairs and the voice of my wife patiently explaining where clothes, books and phones could be found. Doors were never closed and lights and heaters never turned off, which resulted in shocking electricity bills, but now there was only heavy silence and darkness throughout much of the house. My world had changed and although I was lucky to have family and friends, they would not be with me at breakfast or when watching television alone at night. Retirement should have allowed us to spend the rest of our days together, but now I would be spending that time alone.

My wife always cooked meals and I knew which hob to use to boil my egg but had no idea how to operate the two ovens or set the timer and heat controls. My wife never needed the instruction booklet, but I certainly did. Lights glowed and the fan whirred, but the result was still underdone or overcooked food. Fortunately, there was a cookery book for the microwave oven explaining how to cook fish, chicken, steak and even bake potatoes. Carrots and potatoes needed washing and messy scraping, but supermarkets did a range of frozen vegetables, which only needed heating in the microwave. It could also heat up my coffee if it went cold when I was reading microwave cooking instructions. The washing machine also gave me problems. My wife opened the door, tossed in bundles of dirty clothes and washing powder, dialled the programme and walked away. It all looked so simple, a child could do it. When I was finally forced to do my first giant wash, I loaded in a pile of dirty clothes, added powder, chose a programme and went off to do the housework. After returning and unloading the washer, my tennis whites were tennis blues. Fortunately, my daughters gave me guidance on separating whites and colours and choosing appropriate wash programmes. Both daughters called regularly and it was best to allow them to clear my wife's wardrobe and clothing drawers, which spared me the anguish.

Acquaintances who had lost partners assured me that time would heal my loss and help me to adapt and rebalance my life, whilst still cherishing the happy memories. I knew I should get involved in as many activities as possible to leave no time to feel lost or bitter about the giant gap in my life. I was fit and healthy and able to live comfortably on my income. Having worked long hours in my job and spent many nights away from home, most of my free time had been taken up with my family. I had few leisure pursuits but played golf and tennis whenever I could.

As time passed, I noticed that surfaces in the house were coated with dust. Since the doors and windows were mostly closed, it was strange how so much dust had found its way inside. While I was away during the day, my wife must have spent hours battling with dust creeping in through the letterbox, chimney and any small openings. Watching my daughter draw her finger along a dusty windowsill, I felt guilty and set up a routine to clean one or two rooms each week. They would be dusted and windows and carpets cleaned. It soon dawned on me that much of my time was taken up with cleaning and maintaining a house with seven rooms, when I used only three. I slept in my bedroom, cooked in the kitchen and relaxed in the lounge. It was time to move to a smaller, more manageable, property.

During my wife's illness the garden was neglected and the house really needed brightening up. I began by redecorating all the rooms, which kept me busy for three months and luckily the windows, doors and weatherboards were plastic and needed little maintenance. The front and back gardens were overgrown and clearing weeds and replanting took another month, but the house was now looking bright and attractive and was ready for sale. I made sure that I was available to meet every interested buyer and used every opportunity during the inspection to sell the ample space and pleasant location of the house. The sale price was at the top end of the estate agent's estimate which showed my hard work had paid off. After checking local estate agents lists, I found a small two years' old three-bedroom town house with a basement garage in my neighbourhood. It was on an attractive estate, quite near my friends, convenient for access by bus and perfect for my needs. Clearing surplus furniture and belongings accumulated over thirty years proved a major problem. Every room, the attic and every cupboard seemed to be filled. The new owner agreed to buy the garden furniture and other items in the garden shed and keep the trays, fertilisers and sundries in the greenhouse. After allowing family and friends to choose items, a local trader agreed to remove the remainder. I bought new furniture to suit the smaller rooms in my new home and moved in to begin my new life.

The change from my large detached house to a townhouse left me with a healthy bank balance, which was invested in shares giving me good dividends to supplement my income. The new house had a small rear garden, which was mainly paved and with little maintenance needed; there should be plenty of free time to try new experiences and make new friends. There was also a short drive with an overgrown lawn alongside. Since my lawnmower had been left with the new owner of my detached house, I decided to dig up the front lawn and pave it over.

To save time, one kitchen cupboard was reserved for a mug, three plates, knife, fork and spoon which I used every day. These were washed and put back after each meal to avoid building a clutter of dirty dishes, which I had seen in a bachelor friend's house. Being in the habit of wandering around the house when drinking coffee, I often found my cup in the strangest places and appreciated just how much time my wife must have spent collecting and returning crockery, clothes and other items to their proper places. The townhouse had a built-in dishwasher in the kitchen, but there was no need to use it with my limited use of dishes and cutlery. Also, there was no instruction book. My neighbours were friendly and I began looking forward to building a new life as a single man. There were curtain rails fitted over most windows but no curtains, and I chose bright materials when ordering from a local store. Until they arrived, I had to crouch down every time I passed in front of my bedroom window in my jockey shorts. I wanted to avoid having any passing neighbour see an unclothed new resident on the estate. The dawn daylight flooding my bedroom each morning woke me very early and I was usually the first customer at the local newsagents. Since it was now only a ten-minute drive to my golf club, I began playing a round most mornings after driving off the first tee at 7.30 am. I had the course to myself and could take my time safe from other golfers hitting their ball when I was still within range of their reckless strokes. Sometimes other early golfers would join me, but I was happy to play alone and compete against the course by putting the ball in the hole in a specified number of strokes.

My first local contact was with Rod, the owner of The Yorkshireman pub, which would now be my local and fortunately, it was only a short walk from my new home. He and his wife, Rachel, ran the pub and while she looked after the catering, Rod was in charge of the bar. They were a charming couple who had worked hard to build the business after buying it from a brewery, which failed to make sufficient profit. The estate later expanded and the pub was now profitable and very popular with local residents. Rod was able to give me the phone number of a window cleaner and direct me to the nearest supermarket and newsagent. Of all the advice given to me, the most convincing was that of the greenkeeper, who looked after the cricket pitch and bowling green at the local sports ground. He lost his wife after forty years of marriage and told me that there were many partners who suffered for years in a bad marriage, which they only wanted to forget. I was lucky to have enjoyed a good marriage and would always have pleasant memories to look back on as I began to live the rest of my life. I was determined to make a success of my remaining years, both for my family and myself. After the bereavement, sale of my house and dramatic change in lifestyle, I began to feel hopeful about my new role as a senior single.

Chapter 2
Spanish Lessons

I booked a course to learn Spanish at the local college, which was held every Monday afternoon. There were eighteen students but only six were men, which could be a reflection of the amount of personal free time available or the urge to learn a foreign language. During our first coffee break, we began to introduce ourselves and then the ladies gathered in a noisy group in one corner to discuss the failings of their men and their problems with their children. The men sat quietly drinking their coffee and flicking through the dated magazines scattered around. Fred, who was sitting next to me, introduced himself. He had carefully combed the hair on the right side of his head so that it stretched across the top to meet hair similarly combed over from the left side. Unfortunately, it still left an area in the middle with his shiny scalp exposed. He was coughing regularly and between coughs and in a gruff voice, he managed to tell me.

"The fags are killing me and my wife keeps telling me to give them up, but since she's been on the change, they are the only pleasure I have left."

Charlie on my other side heard this and told us that after having their second child, his wife started wearing knickers reinforced with steel thread to keep herself in and him out. They both looked expectantly at me to hear if I had any similar marital problems and were startled by my response.

"My wife died and I am now a widower living on my own."

Charlie rubbed his stubbled chin, blew his nose, grinned at me and then offered me his own advice.

"Oh man. You can pick and choose and they will all be offering you their charms until one of them gets your ring on her finger."

"I quite like living on my own."

Fred was not impressed and wanted to add his views on the dangers and opportunities for a single man.

"You won't be allowed to stay single for long. Once they know you are available, they will all be doing everything they can to get you into their marriage union. See, it unsettles the men they control seeing someone free to enjoy himself and you become a threat and a challenge to all the ladies. Still, can't be bad with every day a honeymoon for you so long as you can stay free."

Knowing I could not win, I changed the subject and asked them why they had signed up to learn Spanish. They both told me that it would get them out of the house and they would be able to impress their friends when they were on holiday on the Costa Blanca in Spain. Listening to my two dismal fellow students, l thought how lucky I had been to have a wife who was my best friend, lover and companion. We were a mixed age group, with the average around fifty years of age. After the first few weeks, we had begun to identify the extroverts and shy characters amongst the group and form friendships. The ladies tended to be more personal in their questions and once one woman had learned that I was a widower, they all knew, including our vivacious Spanish tutor, Anita.

Having changed my life to give myself lots of free time, when we were given work to do at home, such as building our vocabulary or learning irregular verbs, I made sure the work was done since there were no other interests to distract me. To my surprise, I soon became the star pupil and Anita regularly singled me out during the lessons, which embarrassed me and was also noticed by the other students. The ladies began teasing me about being favoured and one told me to watch my step, since Anita had no husband. Whilst courting as a teenager all those years ago, the men were usually the predators and the ladies waited to be approached or propositioned. Now the tables had turned giving me the feeling that I was the one being pursued. Anita was an attractive woman but twenty years younger than me. Perhaps she was just lonely and had got to the stage when she was willing to consider almost anyone as a husband.

During our coffee breaks, Anita began sitting beside me and telling me about her time as a singer in a travelling group and how she had been performing in Valencia and met her Spanish husband. She gave birth to a baby girl and her husband took a job in Barcelona and left her with no money to pay the rent, which meant she had either to support herself and the baby or go back to Yorkshire. After borrowing the money to buy flight tickets, she returned home to live with her parents in Leeds, but during her marriage, she had learned to speak Spanish. She went back to college to gain the necessary qualifications and was now teaching Spanish to mature students. It must have been very difficult for her to survive such callous behaviour by her husband and build herself a new career as a single mother. She was very sympathetic about my loss and wanted to know how I was managing on my own with the cooking, cleaning and ironing. She was impressed when I told her about selling up and moving house, then organising my household chores. Anita was particularly interested in my plans to visit Las Vegas, and to my amazement, offered to go with me. I panicked and nearly choked on my coffee as I put her off by telling her that it was getting too near Xmas and I was now thinking of going in the New Year. She assured me that she would be quite happy to share a room to keep the cost down. I was amazed that an attractive single woman was offering to go away with me and share a room and possibly a bed. I was medium height, with grey hair and considered myself very average and ordinary. I was a non-smoker, drank very little and enjoyed my food, but was not a big eater. After always being active in sports, golf and tennis kept me reasonably slim and fit.

Thinking about the comment that Anita had no husband made me feel nervous about being singled out as a candidate and prompted me to avoid giving give her any encouragement.

The coffee break was late finishing and as a result, the afternoon lesson also finished late. Anita apologised to us and said that she had now lost her lift and would have to walk to the station. A female voice from the back of the class suggested that I could give her a lift. Before I could think of an excuse for refusing, Anita had given me a big smile and accepted. I was sure the offer made on my behalf was by the same woman who had warned me that Anita had no husband. This made me more anxious to avoid having the woman's sense of humour encourage more advances from Anita. At the car park, I opened the passenger door for Anita and she beamed at me and said BMWs were her favourite cars. Things were not going to plan and I had somehow to cool Anita's growing enthusiasm and attention. At the railway station, I stopped the car and kept the engine running as I stayed inside and kept well over to the driver's side as Anita got out. I wanted to be well out of range of any sudden hugs or kisses coming my way. I acknowledged her thanks with a simple wave and drove off.

The following week, the coffee-break conversation as Anita sat beside me got longer and I noticed her skirt had got shorter. She had been a dancer as well as a singer and had trim ankles, which were on prominent display. Anxious to avoid another shared car ride, ten minutes before the lesson ended, I excused myself and claimed a dental appointment. My relief when I reached the car park was cancelled out by knowing that I was a wimp, running away from an over friendly divorcee. The following week, we were due to take our oral test to obtain our Spanish certificate. Preserving my new life style was more important to me than getting a piece of paper with my Spanish pass mark and instead I spent exam day shooting with my best friend, Dickie. The weather turned nasty and as we stood on the exposed Yorkshire moor, the rain lashed our faces and strong winds took hold of the clays, which either stopped or accelerated away across the sky. I always enjoy shooting but was glad to clear my gun and hurry back to the car for shelter and to take off my soaked clothing. Even with the car heater on maximum, it was twenty minutes before we both stopped shivering. The bad weather could have been a punishment on me for dodging Anita and my exam.

After returning from the afternoon shoot, I was startled to hear Anita's voice on my answer phone, offering me a second chance to sit the exam by calling at the college the following Monday evening after classes. I guessed that she had found my number on my course application form. Turning things over in my mind, I decided that I should have discouraged Anita at the outset and made it clear to her that I was happy with my lifestyle and would not change. Leaving early and missing the exam test day was foolish. I enjoyed the company of women and would just have to learn how to discourage any who were set on marriage.

I telephoned the college and left a message at reception that I would be at the college at the suggested time of 5.30 pm to take the Spanish oral test. The receptionist assured me that Mrs Moreno would be ready for me. Hearing this, it seemed that my tutor was fairly sure I would respond to her telephone invitation and I would have to explain to her that we were meeting only for the test. When I arrived, I was directed to a room on the third floor and found Anita waiting at the door. There were no other students being tested and Anita must have stayed behind just for me. We sat down at a desk and I responded to her questions in Spanish with my answers in Spanish. The test finished and I was given a pass with 95%, which came as a pleasant but rather suspicious surprise to me. Anita seemed rather subdued and was not her usual chatty self. I asked her if she had any problems and was startled to see her suddenly burst into tears. Between the tears she, told me that she had just found out that her sixteen-year-old daughter was two months pregnant. The girl was clever and Anita wanted her to go on to university and have a better life than she had herself. The baby could ruin everything or her daughter could have an abortion. Anita was Catholic and her daughter was not and had asked her mother to tell her what to do. I listened as Anita voiced her worries and tried to make a decision. Her instincts as a mother and thoughts of the young baby seemed to be her strongest emotions. I had no right to give advice and kept silent and just listened. Anita spoke about all the changes she could make to look after the child, if she decided to insist that her daughter should continue her education. An hour later, I drove Anita to the railway station after she had decided she would have to rearrange her life to cope with her daughter's baby. I explained how I had altered my own life and had no plans to include anyone else and was happy living on my own. Anita gave me a big hug and a kiss with cheeks still wet with tears and I wished her good luck but wisely did not congratulate her on becoming a grandmother. I had decided that I was quite happy with my basic Spanish and would not be taking more lectures. Perhaps I would have trouble understanding the rapid conversation of a native Spaniard, but at least I would be able to greet them, give my name, describe the weather and even order coffee or churros. Heaven help me if the car broke down and I had to buy spares or have it repaired. Luckily, Dickie had a small pocket-sized translator for French and Spanish and perhaps I could borrow it, or even buy one myself before the next holiday on the continent.

Chapter 3
The Cyprus Holiday

It was well into autumn and a good time to convert my lawn into a maintenance-free paved area. I hired a skip and began digging up the scraggy lawn and weeds and shovelling them into the skip. Hot and sweaty, I made myself a coffee and was sitting on my small wall admiring my work when a lady jogger stopped to talk to me.

"Hi, my name is Helen and I live just eight houses up from you. Welcome to the estate and I hope you will be very happy here. Are you laying a new lawn, or have you just given up on this one?"

"Hello and it is nice to meet you, Helen. My name is Tom and I am going to pave it all over, perhaps with the odd space for small shrubs and give up mowing and regular weeding. Although I might just brush it over occasionally."

"Wonderful. That sounds great to me and perhaps I can watch how you do it and then I can do the same to mine, which always looks untidy."

I told her it might take a while for me to complete my work, but if she wanted to do the same, we were only eight houses apart if she needed help. Telling me she might take me up on my offer, she smiled and carried on jogging to her house. Helen seemed very pleasant and friendly and I hoped my other neighbours would be just as friendly when I met them.

My best friend Richard 'Dickie' Chambers was a retired surveyor and long-time divorcee, who always seemed to be enjoying himself in spite of ongoing battles with his bitter ex-wife and only son. She had convinced his son that Dickie was entirely responsible for breaking up the family and home and both never missed an opportunity to be unpleasant to him. An ex-rugby player, he had since lost his hair and his original enthusiasm for sport. Fortunately, he still enjoyed walking, which helped him to keep his weight down to a reasonable level and we often went on the moors together. We both liked clay pigeon shooting and regularly met for coffee, a meal or a drink in our local pub. After a meal one evening, he suggested we book a holiday together. Having spent months of hectic activity involved in selling one house and buying another, as well as disposing of an incredible amount of furniture and belongings, I was more than ready to take a holiday and agreed.

Our holiday choice was Cyprus, which should be pleasantly warm in autumn and thoughts of leaving a wet and windy Yorkshire for sand, sea and sun in the Eastern Mediterranean were soon cheering me up. We booked a three-star hotel near Paphos with half board and flew from Manchester Airport. The hotel had extensive grounds running down to the seafront promenade, with tennis courts, swimming pool, an archery area and table tennis. There was also a walkway at the edge of the beach, which led to the centre of Paphos. Table tennis was very popular with hotel guests and so far, we had only been able to play one game and were trounced by two lads from Liverpool. Most afternoons, Dickie was happy to lie on a sunbed with a book and a drink, but did very little reading. I usually walked along the beach or swam in the large pool before joining him. One afternoon after walking along the beach, I stopped to watch two ladies playing tennis. It was obvious that one could play quite well, but the other looked as if she was not enjoying the game and played badly. The ball was knocked out of court and I picked it up and threw it back. The hopeless player came over to me at the fence, wiped the perspiration from her face and told me it was too hot for her to be playing tennis. To my surprise, she then offered me her racquet and invited me to take her place. I asked the other player if she was happy to let me join her and she waved her racquet at me to come on court.

I was wearing my canvas beach shoes, but was happy to play, and Trudy and Jean introduced themselves. Jean was a good player, but I was in a local club and regularly played league tennis. With greater experience, it was not difficult to keep Jean chasing balls around the court. After twenty minutes under the blazing sun, Jean raised her hands and told me she was too hot to play any longer and needed a drink. She invited me to join her with Trudy for a cold beer as a reward for giving her a good game. We sat together on the terrace and sheltered from the blazing sun under a giant parasol. The ladies told me that they were from York, where Trudy worked part time in an insurance broker's office. She was of medium height and had brown hair and eyes, and was a little overweight around the hips and chest. She always seemed to be smiling and chatting, and laughed easily. Jean had retired from a career in teaching and was a little taller than Trudy and slimmer, with blue eyes and frizzy fair hair. She seemed more serious and a little reserved. Trudy was married with two grown-up children and Jean was divorced and had no children. They had been at school together, lived near each other and often went on holiday or for weekend breaks. Trudy had lots of free time and was often on her own because her husband was a long-distance lorry driver. There was no sign of Dickie and Trudy said she had noticed us at dinner and boldly asked if the two of us were an item. It suddenly dawned on me that two men together on holiday could give that impression. Trudy was smiling as she watched my face and waited for me to answer.

"We have known each other a long time and I am a widower and my friend Dickie is a retired surveyor and is divorced. We spend a lot of our time together, are in the same gun club, go shooting and walking and have an occasional meal or drink. This is the first time we have been on holiday together, but I just sold one house and moved to something smaller and a Cyprus holiday sounded very tempting to me."

Trudy gave me a big smile and turned to wink at Jean.

"You were right, Jean, and my big mouth has let me down again. My kids have grown up and my hubby now spends more time in his lorry than he does with me, so whenever we can, Jean and I go out together."

Just then, Dickie appeared and seemed surprised to find me sitting with two ladies but wasted no time in joining us. He had a very red face and legs and explained that he had been sitting in the shade, fallen asleep and woke up in full sun to find that he had been burned. He had gone up to our room to apply cream to ease the pain. I introduced the two ladies, who startled us with their personal explanations. Jean spoke first.

"I used to teach at a local college and generally had a lot of marking and other work to do at night. My husband was not happy about this and usually went out and let me get on with it. One night, he went out and never came back, so we got divorced and now that I am retired, I just want to enjoy the rest of my life."

Trudy nodded her head and spoke about her own relations in her marriage.

"I used to hate it when my husband went off in his lorry to deliver to the continent and I did all the decorating and gardening to keep our home nice for him. One day, I decided to give his lorry cab a good clean out and found a pair of knickers down the side of the seat. They were not my size or colour, and I guessed that my man must have been enjoying company when he was away in his little cab. When I asked him how they got there, he was taken by surprise and looked really guilty. He claimed that he had stopped at a motorway café to eat and it was pouring with rain and a woman begged him for a lift. She was soaking wet and he let her change her clothes in his cab and she must have dropped her knickers. I told him that she had dropped her knickers all right, but not because they were wet. After that I made up my mind that if he could enjoy himself, then so could I."

I watched as Dickie suddenly seemed to forget about smoothing his sunburned legs and hang on every word spoken by Trudy. After standing and saying that he would get more drinks, he turned back and made a suggestion.

"Well, girls, I am no tennis player, but I do like walking and dancing and music, and we have most of our holiday still to go, so why don't we all get together?"

The ladies were happy to agree, because although they were enjoying the sunshine, they told us that the entertainment in the hotel was poor and at the end of their first week, they had already seen all the local attractions and were getting bored. Dickie came back with our drinks and we began chatting and considering what to do for their last week. I suggested hiring a car so that we could drive off after breakfast each day and visit the Troodos Mountains and the beaches along the coast. Once we had all agreed, the group broke up to change for dinner after we arranged to meet at 7 pm to share a table together. The hotel operated a buffet service, which suited me because I like flavour rather than bulk and could choose just what I wanted. Inevitably, some of the guests piled up their plates and even went back for more to make sure that they got full value for their money. It was a lovely evening and as we were drinking our coffee in the lounge, Trudy told us she needed some fresh sea breezes and Dickie was going to take her on his favourite walk along the promenade. After they left, Jean asked if I would like a walk after our tennis game and we went off in the opposite direction. Nothing was said about choosing a different walk, but we both realised that Trudy wanted to spend time with Dickie. I noticed that we had quietly separated into two couples.

We stood together at the seawall and watched the waves and the sun setting over the old stone fort in Paphos. It had been a slow walk to allow us to look at the shops and restaurants along the promenade. Checking my watch, I found that it was ten o'clock and suggested I get drinks so that we could sit at an outside table and watch the velvet black sky, which seemed to be filled with stars. Jean was surprisingly easy to talk to and we were both relaxed in each other's company. To my surprise, Jean asked about my wife and at first, I found it difficult to describe the great times we had enjoyed together. Then I became concerned that I was being morbid and apologised for boring her. Jean put her hand on my arm and spoke to me:

"Tom, you are not boring me, quite the reverse. You had a good marriage and I did not and wonder what might have been if I had met the right man. Listening to you, I feel sad about what I missed in my life, but now I just want to make my retirement as enjoyable as possible."

We spoke about our jobs and Jean was envious of the foreign travel involved with my work. I told her that at first, I found it exciting, but when I was flying or driving off on Sunday as other families were relaxing together, I gradually began to tire of the glamour and instead wished I could spend every weekend at home with my own family. Had I not been prepared to accept the need to sacrifice my family time, my career would not have been as successful. As we walked back to the hotel, Jean took my arm and it seemed so natural. I saw her as a pleasant and attractive woman, who was good company, but I still felt married and a little guilty over being with her. At the hotel we used the lift together, but were on different floors. As she was leaving after reaching her floor, Jean put her arms on my shoulders and kissed me on the cheek. I felt relieved because I liked Jean but thought that I was not ready yet for a serious relationship and Jean seemed to have realised this too. Back in my room, there was no sign of Dickie and I suspected that he and Trudy were really enjoying each other's company. There had been too much misery and too little happiness in my friend's life and I was glad they were getting along so well. I always wake early in the morning and I saw that Dickie was lying on his bed fast asleep and snoring loudly into the pillow. He was fully dressed and lay on top of the bedclothes. I wondered whether it was due to alcohol, or exhaustion, since he always gave me full details of his many affairs with his ladies. I smiled to myself as I wondered if it had been Trudy's knickers which dropped this time. I went down to breakfast and as I sat down, I was pleased to see Jean smiling at me as she headed for my table. I pulled out a chair for her to sit beside me and spoke to her:

"My friend Dickie is fast asleep and still fully dressed. It must have been a very long walk he took with Trudy."

Jean laughed and told me that Trudy woke her up flushing the toilet after midnight and spread a trail of clothes as she made her way to bed. She left her in bed awake but not yet ready for breakfast. I suggested a swim after breakfast and we were soon in the pool, which was almost empty since most of the guests were either sleeping or eating. I wanted to rent a car and Jean asked if she could come with me. We drove back to the hotel in a small two-door car and found Trudy and Dickie drinking coffee on the terrace. For our first trip, we drove to the Tombs of The Kings. The site was two miles west of Paphos and we explored the stone ruins of the enormous burial ground, which was used first by the Greeks and then the Romans. There were still some almost intact stone pillars and underground galleries but walking over the rough surfaces under the blazing sun soon became very tiring and we left to find a cafe and cold drinks.

After a light midday snack, we drove east towards Larnaca to visit Aphrodite's rock and cave. The goddess of love was said to have bathed in the pool near the cave and legend has it that swimming in the water brings eternal youth, but the sheer rocks are dangerous and bathing there is strictly forbidden. Perhaps it was just as well, because I could not imagine spending life as a permanent teenager and my youth was now well behind me. We drove on to Pissouri and parked near the attractive beach to relax on the warm sand. After soaking up enough sun, we walked into the village for ice cream and then drove back to our hotel. During the rest of the week, we drove around the Troodos Mountains, visited three monasteries and the memorial to Archbishop Makarios, who had been the Greek Cypriot leader. Unfortunately, he was also the leader of the terrorists killing British soldiers in his illegal campaign to make Cyprus part of Greece.

Each evening, Trudy and Dickie went off together and Jean and I either walked, or drove to pleasant locations, or vantage points, where we could watch the sunset, or the spectacular evening skies. We walked arm in arm and enjoyed being together as we talked about our lives, our jobs and even our school times. I sensed that Jean was waiting for me to take our relationship a stage further but understood that having lost my wife just over a year ago, my feelings were still raw.

It was the last day of their holiday and the girls would be flying back to Leeds Bradford Airport the next morning. They suggested we go out for dinner as their treat for making their holiday so enjoyable. They chose the restaurant and we ordered Meze, which is a ten-course delivery of traditional Greek dishes, probably their equivalent of the Spanish tapas meals. Dickie and I chose the white and red wines to go with the dishes as our contribution to the evening and we left the car at the hotel because we wanted to drink wine with the meal. After working our way through the steady flow of courses, we walked the short distance back to our hotel and sat down in the lounge to rest up and order coffees. Dickie popped up to our room for some tissues and the girls went off to powder their noses. When they returned, Trudy suddenly pulled Dickie to his feet and insisted that they take a last walk near the sea. As Jean and I drank our coffee, I had a feeling that she wanted to speak to me about something and was obviously nervous. Finally, she finished her coffee and took my hand.

"Thank you for making this holiday so very special for us. Since this is our last night here, I want to ask you to do something for me."

There was a long pause and my mind was busy anticipating all sorts of possible requests and situations. Then Jean seemed to decide on her next words.

"I don't know whether you know this, but Dickie doesn't really live up to his name."

Seeing my startled look, she took a deep breath and carried on speaking.

"Trudy is a very physical and impetuous person and she finds Dickie kind and gentlemanly. He makes her laugh and has a knack of helping her to feel special, which is a rare feeling for her. She still lives with her husband, but they lead separate lives and do not sleep in the same bed since the knickers incident. We go away together so that she has some enjoyment in her life, because she has none at home. They watch us go for our evening walk and return to our bedroom for sex. Unfortunately, although they both want to make love, Dickie has a problem. As Trudy puts it, he needs a couple of splints for support. Dickie blames this on not having had sex for some time and Trudy has been helping him and thinks she is now almost able to solve his problem. She would like to swap rooms for tonight so that she and Dickie can make a last attempt."

Jean paused and watched my face closely as she waited for my reaction.

"Wow, Jean, that comes as a bit of a shock to me. Dickie is always telling me about his success with women and I assumed he was enjoying a very active sex life. You and I have already seen each other in our swimsuits, so if we share a room, you won't embarrass me in your pyjamas."

"I don't wear pyjamas and I am certainly not going to bed in my swimsuit. I will keep my underwear on to save embarrassing you if you are willing to swap rooms."

"In this hot weather, I always sleep with no clothes on at all and generally lie on top of the sheets, but I can wear my boxer shorts tonight. I know how upset Dickie would be if I ruined his plans because I wouldn't share a room with you."

"Trudy would be disappointed as well because she really likes your friend. He has your room key and I have the key of our room. He has moved your shaving and toothbrush bag to our room so that you have everything you need in the morning. He warned me that you are an early riser and is hoping you will agree to the move for our last night. Please don't think I am doing this just to get you to go to bed with me. Trudy is my best friend and I would do anything for her. I never wear pyjamas or anything else, but tonight as I said, I will keep my underwear on. I expect it will be uncomfortable, but it will be helping Trudy and your friend. I think all that food and wine has made me sleepy and I am ready for bed now, if you are happy to go up to our room. They will go to your room when they get back from their walk."

As we went up together in the lift, I had butterflies in my stomach and could not believe I was going to bed with a woman I had only met six days ago, even though it was to help Dickie. Once in the hotel room, Jean invited me to use the bathroom first as she moved Trudy's clutter from the room and bedside table. It was hot in the room and the air conditioning was so noisy that we agreed to switch it off. After cleaning my teeth, I lay on top of the sheets and waited for Jean to join me in the double bed, which had come as a bit of a surprise. I thought about the two single beds in my room and how cramped one would be for two people, then realised that was part of the attraction for Dickie. I could not help myself and watched as Jean came from the bathroom in her bra and panties, which had a noticeable effect on me. Embarrassed, I turned on my side and sank my head in the pillow. Jean got into bed beside me and switched the light off. Just as I was drifting off to sleep, I heard Jean muttering and felt her moving about behind me. I lifted my head and asked if she was OK.

"I am just taking this damned bra off, or I will never get to sleep because it is so uncomfortable to lie on. Sorry if I woke you."

It had been a full day and with no car to drive, I had drunk more than my usual half glass of wine and quickly fell asleep. In the early hours, I woke to go to the toilet, remembered to put the seat back down and made sure I did not disturb Jean. She was lying face down and spread-eagled on top of the sheets, with one breast peeping out from under her arm. I usually leave a small gap in the curtains to know when it is daytime and when I woke, I could see the bright blue Cyprus sky through the opening. I vaguely remembered having a pleasant dream, but as usual could not recall the details. Checking my watch, I saw that it was still only just after six o'clock. It was certainly cooler in the early morning, but my back felt pleasantly warm with the soft touch of Jean's breasts pressed against me, while her arm lay across my waist with her hand on my stomach. I could feel her warm breath on the back of my neck and then a voice in my ear whispered, "Good morning," but neither of us made any effort to get up. I began to get an erection and suddenly thought that I might reach Jean's hand. I tried to lie still, but it was becoming more and more difficult trying not to move. I knew that soon I would either have to get up or turn to face Jean. I could stand it no longer and turned around and Jean kissed me slowly on the mouth.

We all met for breakfast and Trudy and Dickie were in cheerful mood. Jean smiled at me and mouthed 'success' as she put her hand on my knee and squeezed. We saw them to their coach and exchanged addresses so that we could meet up some time. Jean put her arms around me and gave me a long kiss on the mouth, then invited me to visit York one day to play tennis at her club. She slipped a piece of paper into my hand and I saw her name and telephone number written on it. Dickie noticed and asked me if I had given her my telephone number and I told him no. He and Trudy had exchanged addresses, but she warned him that sometimes her husband answered the phone and it would be safer to pass messages through Jean. I asked him if he planned to keep in contact with Trudy, but he said that it was too soon for him to decide, but he thought she was great company and he was very tempted.

It had simply not occurred to me to give Jean my phone number and thinking about it, I guessed it was because I still had my instincts as a married man, but it had not prevented me enjoying my night with Jean, or the days we spent in each other's company. Nevertheless, I was still nervous about making new relationships as I began my new life style. During the Cyprus holiday, I had gained a new friend and York was not so far away.

Chapter 4
U3A

After our Cyprus holiday, I noticed a marked reluctance by my friend Dickie to describe his current activity with local ladies. During the flight back from Cyprus, I expected him to talk about our last night with Jean and Trudy from York, particularly since it involved having us swap rooms and moving me into bed with Jean. I also hoped to hear something about his help from Trudy and whether she had succeeded in curing his problem. His silence convinced me that it was due to embarrassment that I knew about his difficulties and as a result, he said nothing about Trudy and I kept silent about my night with Jean.

As we landed at Manchester Airport, I looked out at the rain driving against my window and shivered, then told Dickie that I might be interested in any more holiday ideas, he could come up with which took us where the weather was dry and warm. We had booked a taxi and were soon on our way home through very light traffic as we crossed over the Pennines, because it was still only 7 am. I was dropped off first and rushed to switch the heating on, then worked my way through the accumulated mail. By nine o'clock, the rain and mist had cleared away and it was time to get the car out and get some food in. Outdoor sport was out of the question, but for some time, I had been thinking about yoga, which was supposed to keep joints and body muscles in good working order. A friend had told me about the University of the Third Age and since I was just past middle age, more or less, I was sure I would be eligible. The local branch had over 2,000 members and offered a range of sporting tuition, keep fit classes, foreign language tuition and other courses at very modest charges. There were vacancies in the badminton and yoga classes and I would have liked to take both, but my free time now appeared to be limited. I enrolled for the Tuesday yoga class starting the following week.

I wondered if Dickie would be interested in any of the U3A courses and rang him to arrange meeting for a pub lunch and chose a table as close as possible to the roaring wood fire. Was the weather getting colder, or was it because I was getting older? Perhaps it was just due to the temperature drop after two weeks of hot Cyprus sun. Dickie read through the list of courses and activities on offer from U3A, but the only one which interested him was bridge, which he could play sitting down. He could not understand why I had signed up for yoga classes and he thought I was mad to lie on the floor and twist myself into all sorts of odd shapes just to get fit.

It was too cold for shorts and I arrived at the old church building in jog pants and top for my first yoga lesson. As my fellow patients filed into the room, I was startled to find myself as the only man in the group, surrounded by eighteen ladies in tight-fitting leotards. Was it only the local ladies who were prepared to twist and bend to improve their muscle and body flexibility? Were the men all on the golf course instead, or was there sport showing on television? The ladies were obviously surprised to see me but were quite friendly and very helpful in giving me advice when my legs or arms were not quite in the most painful position. I was slim and soon adapted to the required contortions, although I felt the strain with some and wondered how I would feel in the morning. I was pleased to find that I could stand on one leg and raise one knee and my arms, then stand poised and triumphant, or so I thought. Some of the ladies could also pose on one leg, but most decided not to try. Many were well over middle age and perhaps due to childbirth and having little time for sports had gained extra weight. For them, achieving the correct yoga pose was quite hard, but they were determined to follow our instructor's guidance. At coffee break time, as a minority of one, I was kept busy answering questions about my home and family. Having tanned arms and face caused comment and I explained that I had just returned from Cyprus. When asked if I had travelled on my own, I mentioned Dickie and before any conclusions could be drawn, I also explained that I was a widower. There were no signs of special interest and I assumed that none of them were interested in finding a husband, which came as a pleasant surprise. They were a really great bunch of ladies and I thought my Tuesday yoga lessons would be good for me and would also be in enjoyable company.

After being loaned a mat on my first visit, for my second, I went fully equipped with my own maroon-coloured pad, which looked ridiculously small and nowhere long enough to take my full body length. I wondered if it was designed only to accommodate doubled up bodies, which would fit nicely. There were surprised faces and murmurings when I joined the class for the second week and I asked April, who was a long-term yoga performer, if I was missing something. After roaring with laughter, she told me that I was not the first man to join the group and find he was the only male, but the others had not appeared again after the first lesson. In minimum clothing, I could imagine how a solitary lady amongst an all-male group would have felt out of place, but I was neither embarrassed, nor intimidated. I had come to be trained and would suffer alongside the ladies. We were beginning to learn the downward-facing dog pose, which involved bending our bodies so that with feet on the ground, we also placed our hands flat on the ground and formed an inverted V, with our bottom at the peak. It seemed to stretch most of my upper and lower body and I was glad my stomach was average size to allow me to bend. Suddenly the room echoed to an enormous fart, as a stomach was compressed and air expelled. This was followed by three quieter farts. Nothing was said and the straining, grunting and farting went on until we had finished our session with the downward-facing dog pose. With my head pointing between my legs, I had no idea who the lead performer had been and everyone had simply carried on bending and farting, but seeing the big smile on April's face, I had my suspicions. Our instructor Carolyn was a very serious person, who had said almost nothing to me on my first visit, but at coffee break on my return session, she chatted to me and told me she was ex-army, unmarried and trying to build herself a new life as a civilian. She was tall and slim, with dark brown hair swept back into a ponytail. I guessed that she would be in her mid-forties. Having heard from the usual group chatter that I was a widower, she asked how I was coping now that I was living on my own. I explained the changes I had made with my lifestyle and she was impressed.

She asked if I fancied meeting her for a drink one evening and since it seemed a natural invitation between two single people remaking their lives, I told her it would be fine. Perhaps if she had offered to go away with me, or share a room, I might have seen the possible implications, but I was in good company and enjoying the efficient way she looked after us. The following week after my third yoga lesson, as I was unlocking my car door, I saw Carolyn wave and begin walking towards me and stood waiting for her. Arriving alongside me, she asked if I could help her.

"The brakes on my car are being fixed but it's not ready yet, so any chance of giving me a lift to Morley?"

It would have been churlish of me to refuse and I had no fixed plans for the evening and told her to jump in. It was the middle of the afternoon and the traffic was light so that we arrived at her apartment block in less than thirty minutes. After thanking me, Carolyn invited me in for a coffee and I tried to put her off by telling her about my usual meeting with Dickie for our evening pub meal, but she insisted on showing her appreciation for saving her a long bus ride. Her apartment was on the second floor, with a small hall, kitchen, sitting room and I guessed, one bedroom. We sat and drank our coffee and she told me that she had been a physical training instructor in the army until she returned to civilian life a year ago. She asked me how I spent my leisure time, apart from the yoga. I explained that golf and tennis took up most of my week, whilst shooting, or holidays with my friend Dickie filled the rest. Carolyn was surprised that I had no lady friends to make up for the loss of my wife. I told her that many of my golf and tennis partners were ladies and friends and I had very little free time remaining.

"So you have no regular girlfriend or partner to spend your evenings with, or for your weekend breaks?"

My husband hunter antennae began to signal me that I was entering a danger zone. I thought it wise to explain that I still felt married and was not yet ready to become regularly involved with a woman. Carolyn smiled at me and put her hand on my knee as she suggested that occasional evenings with a woman would surely be more fulfilling and exciting than a pub meal with a man. The warning signals again flashed in my head and I got to my feet and said that I would have to go if I was to be on time for my evening pub meal. Carolyn smiled again and said that if I had to hurry off, perhaps we could have a meal together sometime soon. She opened the door for me and as we passed close together in the doorway, she put her arms around me, moved her body close against mine and kissed me full on the lips. I was unprepared and unresisting, but she was a really good kisser and I must have responded instinctively. As we drew apart, Carolyn had a look of satisfaction on her face because she knew that I was vulnerable to her charms. As I drove away, I felt sad that I would now have to follow all the other men and fail to turn up for the next yoga class. Thinking about how things had moved in the wrong direction, I knew I would never be able to refuse to help ladies or be rude to them when avoiding any amorous approaches.

It was nearly Xmas and this year, I would be at my youngest daughter's home for Xmas lunch, having spent the previous Xmas with my eldest daughter. My son was working in Australia and would not return for at least another year. Sharing meals with my family was wonderful, but I still missed the special contentment of being with a female companion in my own age group. I had not contacted Jean since she flew back from Cyprus and on impulse, I rang her number. She told me that she had been hoping I would call her, if only for a game of tennis, but after the weeks went by, she thought I had forgotten her.

"There is no way I would ever forget you, Jean. Whenever I see pyjamas, I think of you."

"But you know I don't wear them."

"Exactly."

"What happened to the shy widower I met in Cyprus who had to be persuaded to go to bed with me?"

"I was given good advice and decided that since I am a senior and single, I should make the most of my remaining years and keep in touch with lovely lady tennis players. Perhaps the Cyprus holiday convinced me to take full advantage."

"Oh my, what a smooth talker, but unfortunately our tennis court surfaces are being relayed at the moment and they will be closed for the next month at least."

"OK. So how about a game indoors at a sports club near Leeds?"

"That would be lovely if you can arrange it, so when do you want to play?"

We agreed to meet on the following Monday and then I asked if she would also like to bring an overnight bag and spend the night at the Devonshire Arms at Bolton Abbey. Perhaps we could walk along the Wharf riverside to Grassington village the following morning, have lunch and then walk back. Jean laughed and immediately gave me her answer.

"Having spent weeks ignoring me, now you are propositioning me, but it is still the best offer I am likely to get today and I am looking forward to meeting you again."

Two cars would have been a problem and instead I arranged to meet her at Leeds Railway Station. There were tennis courts, a swimming pool, restaurant and other activities at the sports club and after our two hours of tennis and a coffee, we drove to the hotel near Bolton Abbey. When we had showered and changed for the evening, we were impressed by the dinner menu selection and over the meal, Jean told me that Trudy thought I was a toff. I denied this and said I just had clean habits, disliked pyjamas and didn't smoke or gamble. Jean laughed and said she would have to call me Mister Moderation but promised to explain the difference to Trudy. We continued teasing each other over dinner and after coffee in the lounge, went up to our room. It had been a very pleasant day and I was glad I had been able to persuade Jean to meet me again.

Jean was first in the bathroom and came out wearing shiny pink pyjamas, which took me completely by surprise. She laughed at the expression on my face and told me it was my turn for the bathroom. When I got into bed beside her, Jean snuggled up and told me that if I disliked pyjamas so much, I could always take them off. I did. The weather was cold but dry the next morning and we both enjoyed the walk to Grassington, where we had lunch at another Devonshire inn. Jean lived at Haxby on the Wetherby side of York and I drove her home and stayed for coffee and sandwiches. As she was busy in the kitchen, I used my car tool kit to fix her letterbox, which was hanging off on one screw. Jean saw what I was doing and thanked me before telling me how nice it was to have a man around the house and could she give me a list. She also told me I was welcome to stay the night and laughed when I suggested that it might ruin her local reputation.

"It would actually help my reputation to show how an old lady like me can pull a flash fellah in a BMW."

I laughed but did not accept her offer. Staying overnight in her home would move our relationship to a closer level, but I still had things to do and places to see before considering a relationship leading to a permanent commitment. We both enjoyed meeting and having fun together and perhaps we could meet now and again as friends and lovers, without getting too involved. It would suit me, but perhaps it would be unfair on Jean, who might also be looking for a husband. She lived alone and welcomed my help in fixing her letterbox, but I knew there were other maintenance jobs requiring work at her bungalow. She had also invited me to stay the night and perhaps was hoping our casual friendship would become permanent, which I knew I was not ready to take on. At our next meeting, I would have to discuss this with Jean to be sure that I was not being unfair to her. If she did want some sort of commitment from me, I would miss her, but it was just too soon for me to take that step.

When I was back at my house cleaning my car, I finally met the local window cleaner and we agreed that he would call each month since I had no ladders and would let him keep my windows clean. Mine was an end of terrace house and there was a narrow side entrance and gate, which I never locked. If he called when I was out, I told him to put a bill in my letterbox to be paid on his next visit. I was pleased to meet him and made him a cup of tea as he gave me a surprising amount of detail about my neighbours and asked about my own background, presumably to be able to pass my details on to the rest of his customers. He could be a useful source of local knowledge for me, as well as a reliable means of passing information on to my neighbours.

Chapter 5

Along the Nile

I had just put the car in the garage after driving home from York, when the phone rang and it was Dickie inviting me to the local pub for a drink. He told me that he had something really special he wanted to talk about. Walking down to The Yorkshireman pub, I wondered if he had news about Trudy or about some other gorgeous woman he had just met. He was sitting at a corner table with two full glasses of real ale just waiting to be picked up. We usually drank Timothy Taylors beer, which had a good flavour and was not too strong. Before I had taken my first sip, he had already begun to tell me about his latest idea.

"I have always wanted to see the pyramids and sail up the Nile in Egypt and I have just found this company offering two weeks holiday and it is for singles like us only."

It was not a bad suggestion, but there could be cause for concern if two bachelors like us went off on a two-week holiday with single people. I told him we should be very careful.

"Perhaps only single people go on a singles' holiday, but have you thought about being surrounded wherever we go by designing females determined to bring home a husband at the end of the holiday or demand a refund. Or perhaps most of them would be young keep fit fanatics who could kill us off when we try to keep up with them."

Dickie assured me that we would travel with others in our same age group and we would just have to stay close to each other when we were under attack by husband-hunter ladies. Having never been to Egypt and since the holiday would be two weeks in hot sun instead of Yorkshire in freezing cold, it did sound very appealing. As soon as I said I was interested, Dickie produced the brochure and we chose our two weeks, which he would book the next day. The holiday included time in Cairo, Aswan, Luxor and a Nile cruise, all on half board. We would be back in good time to enjoy our usual low key and incredibly quiet life style over Xmas and New Year. In my spare time, I could even work on Jean's to-do list at her house. The previous New Year's Eve, I spent alone at home watching a host of Scottish dancers and bagpipers in kilts squeezing the life out of a cat inside a tartan bag with its tail hanging down. Dickie always seemed to have got himself a lady friend over the year-end holiday period. I assumed that after being divorced for some years, he made sure that he always had female company to brighten up his holiday.

We were advised to have injections to protect us against yellow fever, lockjaw and malaria in Egypt, but it was hard work persuading Dickie that it was necessary. We also learned that sterling was accepted and that there were Egyptian pounds, but of much less value than our own. Dickie had ridden horses at one time and told me he might try having a ride on a camel. I warned him that camels spit at you and also have a nasty habit of turning their heads around to use their enormous teeth to bite their riders. With his legs spread over the camel's back, I warned him that his prospects would be in danger. Dickie immediately decided that camel rides were too dangerous to risk such serious injury. He never knew when I was teasing him, which was probably why I kept doing it. The temperatures in Egypt would be around seventy degrees. It would not be too hot for us as we walked over the sand and rocks and we could pack our normal summer clothes to wear and include plenty of mosquito spray.

The flight from Manchester to Cairo took well over seven hours and from the airport, a bus took us straight to our hotel where we arrived in late afternoon. Once again males were in the minority and as Dickie had claimed, everyone was generally in our age group. We had a very lively lady to look after us as we travelled and to lead us on each day's activities. Her name was Monica and she was about twenty years younger than me and told me she was divorced and lived in my neighbourhood. Since she did not say exactly where she lived, I assumed that she was happy to remain unattached and was not a threat. Dickie and I arrived together and we spent most of our time together, which made it likely that we would again be regarded as an item. Dickie was quite annoyed when I explained but could see the benefit of being protected from any really determined ladies in the husband hunt. We could now choose our contacts, instead of being pursued. For both the ladies and men, the decision to take a singles' holiday was probably made because they were widowed, divorced or just single and hoping to meet someone who might make their lives more enjoyable. When chatting with some of the other guests, I was surprised to learn that for most, this was their first singles' holiday. I wondered if this was because of successful prior holiday pairings with no need for a repeat, or previous disastrous contacts by those who did not want a repeat.

We spent three days in Cairo and for me the museum was the highlight of the holiday. When we were at the pyramids at Giza, we were offered a camel ride and I told Dickie I would take his photograph when he was up in the saddle, but he would not be persuaded. Instead, we stood in front of the squad of looming beasts and the camel herder took our photograph and indicated that we should pay him. Dickie was happy to oblige after avoiding the threat to his prospects, but the herder was not happy to receive Egyptian pounds. The pyramids at Giza were impressive and looking at the size of the stone blocks extending to the very peaks, the ancient Egyptians must have been both skilled craftsmen and outstanding builders. In the Cairo Museum, the incredible treasures found in the tomb of Tutankhamun were on centre display, including his striking gold head mask, a chariot and furniture. Not happy with the two-hour morning visit arranged for tour guests, I went back again during our free afternoon. When I left, Dickie was resting with a book and a drink near the hotel swimming pool under a large canopy. I returned to the hotel and found everyone gathered near the pool playing table tennis. Dickie was playing a muscular lady named Eva from the London area and she was giving him a hard game, which she eventually won to his annoyance. Someone told me she had not lost a game so far. Eva was one of the younger ladies and she always turned up beside us when Dickie and I boarded a coach, sat down for a meal or when Monica arranged an evening dance. Eva told us she had been married to a much older man, who had recently died and she now lived alone in a large house north of London. She described a walled garden with lots of big trees and how she had nursed her ailing husband for his last eight years. Eva was solidly built with thick jet-black hair and signs of a moustache on her upper lip. We were convinced she had her sights set on one of us and each of us hoped it was the other.

After losing his game, Dickie sat down beside me and apologised for letting Yorkshire down. We had a table tennis table in my company office, which was used most lunch times to relax. Status meant nothing and each game was played to win and during my long career, I reached a good standard. Eva walked up to us and asked me to play and Dickie told her to be gentle with me. She completely ignored him and anxious to dispose of another victim, simply inclined her head towards the table. From the moment we began playing, Eva hit out at every ball and just edged the first game, which brought a satisfied smile to her lips and a groan from Dickie. I decided to try a little spin to test her response and the ball just edged away from Eva's bat each time and she knocked it into the net or off the table. She was obviously unused to spin and for the next two games, I let her win a few points and then took points back with heavy spin shots to slow or bend the ball so that she began to get frustrated and careless. After just edging ahead near the finish to win the next two games, I won the set and Eva showed her annoyance by throwing her bat on the table and walking off. She was not popular with the other ladies, who now insisted on buying me a drink. My reputation was made and two ladies in the group began giving me friendly smiles.

Janice came from Bridgend in Wales and was a widow who had shed three stones in weight after her husband died and now had a new wardrobe of close-fitting dresses which emphasised her slim figure. Her husband had been overweight and diabetic and died suddenly at work from a heart attack. Her children had grown up and like me she was making a new life on her own. Pat was my age and a retired hospital administrator from St Helier, who had been divorced for fifteen years and was about to retire. She had no children and was not looking forward to giving up her busy working life and many colleagues. Pat married young and had a good marriage until her husband took to gambling, which led to them having to sell their house to clear his debts. She divorced her husband and worked hard to save for her own house and gain promotion in her work. Both ladies admitted that they would like to find the right man to share their lives and were taking their first singles' holiday.

The Sphinx was not as big as I expected and the nose was badly damaged. The guide told us that when Napoleon invaded Egypt, his soldiers used the nose for target practice. His ships were then used for target practice at the Battle of the Nile won by our Lord Nelson. We flew to Aswan to see the magnificent Aswan Dam financed by the nationalisation of the Suez Canal, owned by Britain and France. Built to hold back the mighty Nile, it controls the flow of water needed throughout the year for crops and ended the annual floods, which previously devastated the surrounding area. At Aswan, we boarded a large steamer to spend four days sailing up the river. Most rivers flow south, but the Nile flows north to its delta at Alexandria in the Mediterranean Sea. It begins in Uganda and merges with the Blue Nile from Ethiopia just north of Khartoum in Sudan. Our party shared accommodation with a similar sized group of Italians and at dinner they were surprisingly noisy. On our first evening, we were to be entertained by a belly dancer and Dickie insisted on choosing a table at the side of the polished dance area to get a really good view. The British group sat on the right of the dance floor and the Italian on the left. I remembered being pounced on by two lady boys in Chiang Mai in Thailand and was not keen to be in such an exposed spot but was persuaded to join the group. I was sitting with Janice, Eva, Pat and Dickie, with his current lady friend Joan, who was a widow with her own hairdressing salon. When the oriental music started playing, the men looked up expectantly and the ladies went on chatting amongst themselves. A well-built young woman with tawny glistening skin sidled on to the floor dressed only in very small scraps of lace and metal and began gyrating her lissom body as she made her way around the dance floor. She twisted and shivered and I watched fascinated as the tassels on the tips of her well-filled, but totally undersized, bra revolved clockwise. She was barefooted and there were ornaments and little bells on her ankles which shook and tinkled as she moved. Dickie wondered if she could make each tassel move in different directions and I said it was impossible. After her second circuit of the floor, she suddenly stopped alongside our table as I concentrated on looking across the room and pretending to show no interest. Suddenly my arms were gripped and I was pulled out to the floor by a belly dancer. Wherever I put my hands, I found warm bare flesh and was also nervous about treading on her bare feet as we moved around the dance floor. She took hold of my hands and put one across her back and the other on her belly so that I could feel her muscles flexing as she danced. She had some sort of jewel fitted into her navel, which I kept knocking and tried to avoid dislodging with my hand. I learned that her name was Sunita and as she led, I did my best to follow nervously and then began to enjoy the experience. We must have put on a good performance judging by the applause from the audience when we finished, although it came mainly from the British side. I sat down at our table trying hard not to look too smug and noticed that the Italian group were not impressed. Perhaps Sunita should also have danced with an Italian to avoid bruising Italian national pride.

The next act was to be a 'Whirling Dervish' and I had no idea what to expect. A tall male Arab, wearing knee high leather boots and dark trousers, beneath a full skirt in a heavy fabric, walked out. When the music began, he started turning. Slowly at first, then gradually increasing his pace. The heavy skirt began to rise until it formed a perfect ring around his waist as he was spinning his body at an incredible speed and he kept it up for some minutes. He then began to slow his spinning until he finally stood still and bowed to the audience as we clapped. He then walked off and I could not understand how he could stand so still after spinning for so long, since I know that I would have been staggering around and trying to keep on my feet. After a round of drinks, Janice asked me if I fancied a walk on deck and we climbed the stairs and stood at the rail as our ship glided up the Nile. It was a warm evening and we could see scores of lights gleaming on the shore alongside as we passed and there was a full moon in the coal black sky. I stood behind her and put my arms around her waist as we moved along the river. Fortunately, there were no mosquitos, probably because we were moving and in the middle of the river. After a few minutes, Janice turned towards me and after looking at me for a moment, inclined her head away, presumably to avoid being kissed. I guessed that she still felt married and was happy to let her choose her own pace and actions, just as I did.

The following night, there was a dance and having taken the floor first with Pat, I was with Janice when a dance competition was announced. She was wearing a sheer white dress which was so thin and stretched so tightly that the outline of her knickers was clearly showing and seemed to constantly attract my eyes. Every time the music stopped, couples had to rush to step on squares of newspaper spaced out on the floor. After every stop, the papers were reduced in numbers and size. Eventually, there were only two couples remaining on the dance floor and two very small pieces of paper. We had survived, as well as an Italian couple and I noticed that the very glamorous lady was wearing high-heeled stiletto shoes, while her partner wore light leather shoes. I told Janice to be ready to stand on my shoes and hold me very tightly when the music stopped. The moment came and she could not have got any closer. We stood locked together and watched as the Italian man squirmed when a stiletto heel came down on his thin leather shoes. The couple began to sway before staggering off their paper. We had won and the British side clapped furiously, as once again the Italian side remained almost silent. After bowing to our enthusiastic supporters, we were given a bottle of champagne for winning and filled as many glasses as possible amongst fellow guests on surrounding tables. I was pleased we had won, but having Janice pressed so tightly against me was more enjoyable. Eva could not dance and sat glowering at Janice.

Knowing that Janice was cool on deck embraces, I asked Pat if she would like a walk on deck to watch the evening stars and her face brightened, whilst those of Janice and Eva looked glum. Dickie ordered another bottle of wine and carried on charming Joan. Pat took my arm and after walking along the deck, we sat on a bench and as it was cooler by comparison with the hot ballroom, I put my arm around her shoulders. She told me something about her work in Jersey and asked me about my work and family. She would have liked to have children, but after the break up with her husband, she never met anyone she wanted to share her life with. As we parted near our rooms, she put her arms on my shoulders and kissed me on the cheek, then paused before opening her cabin door. I wasn't sure if she was giving me an invitation but did not want to take advantage.

After four days sailing up the Nile, we arrived in Luxor and our hotel was located alongside the river. The first tour was to the incredible temple at Karnak and walking amongst the giant columns and looking up at the stone pillars towering above me, it was difficult to imagine ancient Egyptians first cutting, then transporting the enormous stone blocks. I could not understand how they had then raised them to such heights without having cranes or hydraulics and wondered how many workers had been crushed in the process. I was trying to find a vantage point to take a picture, but the only suitable spot was roped off. After an earlier terrorist attack, there were armed soldiers everywhere and one signalled to me to step inside the restricted area to take my photo. After taking it, he rubbed his hands together to indicate payment and I gave him money. The two major irritations in Egypt were the flies and the beggars. If you bought anything after haggling over the price, you were then asked to give a gratuity because you had received a reduction, which made no sense. At the Valley of the Kings, a beggar followed me from the coach and walked beside me as he persistently tried to sell me a small statue of Nefertiti. I left him on the surface as I went down to visit the tomb of Rameses and in the enclosed area below, a woman was overcome with the oppressive heat and collapsed. We waited for her to be taken to the surface, by which time we were all soaked with perspiration and anxious to get out of the tomb. The Arab was waiting for me and continued trying to sell me the statue as he followed me all the way back to the coach and was then warned off by an armed soldier. When I sat in the coach beside Dickie, the same beggar was outside my window hurling curses at me with pointed hand gestures. Fortunately, they were no better than the crude statue he wanted me to buy and I was unharmed.

At the hotel, I noticed a path leading down to the Nile and decided to investigate. At the bottom, I found myself at a long stone jetty beside the river where four Arab dhows were moored. I seemed to be surrounded by scores of frogs making very loud croaking noises but could see none of them against the black river water. It suddenly occurred to me that it was not a sensible spot to be at night in a foreign country and hurried back up the steps to the hotel. I would visit the jetty again in daylight when there were people around for protection. Music was playing and some of the guests were doing the quickstep as I walked in. Dickie and Joan were dancing and moving well with their arms entwined. Pat was sitting amongst friends and smiled at me when I nodded towards the dancers, nodded back then walked with me onto the floor. She was a good dancer and chatted as we moved around the dance floor. She never criticised others or made any unpleasant comments. I told her I had holidayed in Jersey with my children and she invited me to visit her whenever I had the time. She was a quiet and undemanding lady who would probably be a good and caring wife, but for me, the essential chemistry was missing. Visiting her in Jersey would only send the wrong message.

When we sat down to have coffee, I noticed a noisy group at another table, including Janice, Eva and two of the male guests. Dickie and Joan joined us and when it was time to take to our beds, Dickie said that Janice looked as if she had drunk too much. I was concerned that she would be unable to get back to her cabin and that she might be helped by one of the men and perhaps exploited. Looking across at the group, I could see that Janice was sitting with her elbows on the table and holding up her head with her hands. I said goodnight to Pat and walked over to sit near Janice, who startled me by immediately putting her arms around my neck and kissing me on the lips. She had definitely had too much to drink. Eventually I persuaded her to let me take her to her cabin, which was not popular with one of the men, who began to rise from his chair until I gently, but firmly, pressed him back in his seat. After walking her back to her cabin, I took her inside and she suddenly put her arms around me, kissed me again and then passed out. She had spent a lot of her money on clothes for the holiday and she might yet be sick, so I undid her dress and managed to take it off and hang it in her wardrobe. After rolling the bedcovers back, I heaved her up and onto the bed, closed her door behind me and left.

It was our last day and we had free time in Luxor. After breakfast I walked down to the river jetty and chatted to the captain of one of the dhows moored alongside. He asked if I would like to sail to Banana Island on the Nile and said if I could get ten people, he would take us for £20. Walking back to the pool where most guests were sunbathing, I persuaded Dickie and Joan to take the trip and as the news spread, we soon had twenty passengers. I took names and collected the cash then allocated names to Dhow I and Dhow 2. Our tour guide Monica was intrigued by the guests surrounding me and paid for a seat on Dhow 2. After boarding, we edged out into the Nile and felt the cooling river breeze on our faces. As we began to pick up speed, the enormous bow sail of the dhow filled with wind and the boat surged forward down the wide river. It was a forty-minute sail south to Banana Island, where we were taken through a grove of banana trees to a small wooden café (shack) in the middle of the plantation. We sat around on wooden benches and were given light snacks and small Egyptian bananas. Dickie whispered that there were cobras in Egypt and they could be amongst the trees. I told him to stay on the path, walk quickly and make sure he avoided treading on any. On our way back to the boats, I had difficulty keeping up with him and he was on board by the time I arrived. The captain suggested we have a race and with a following wind the two vessels ploughed through the Nile water with our helmsman controlling the rope tiller by holding it between his toes. Dhow 2 won the race and Dickie raised his arms in triumph, since I was in Dhow 1. Inevitably on our return to the jetty, we were asked to give gratuities to the crew. Later, whilst sitting down alongside the pool with cool drinks, the holiday representative came over and asked if I was trying to take over her job. Monica was only kidding and bought me a drink but still didn't tell me where she lived. A pale-faced Janice appeared and asked if she could talk to me, so we went down to the riverside and sat on a bench. She was nervous and presumably ashamed as she tried to explain her conduct the previous night. She had missed breakfast and the dhow-sailing trip and was obviously feeling sorry for herself.

"I don't drink usually, but we were all together at the table and whatever it was I drank, it tasted nice, but a little sweet. I wanted you to like me and I don't know why I embarrassed myself by turning my head when I thought you were going to kiss me. Then you took Pat on deck after we won that dance and I knew I had spoiled it all and then I missed your trip down the river. When you sat at our table last night, I kissed you because I wanted to and with my legs all wobbly, you helped me to my cabin. After that I can't remember what happened. Did we, you know?"

She looked so embarrassed that I had to resist my first inclination to tease her about taking her to her cabin, undressing her and putting her to bed and simply explained what happened.

"When I got you to the cabin, you threw your arms around me and kissed me, then you passed out. You were lying on the floor in your best dress and I thought you might be sick on it, so I took it off and hung it up, then put you to bed. Your undies were so flimsy, I didn't think I needed to take them off as well."

"What do you mean they were too flimsy to take off? They were very expensive and supposed to be very provocative to men."

"Yes, they might well be when you want them to be, but not when you are unconscious, likely to be sick and unable to choose."

Janice relaxed and laughed before thanking me for not taking advantage. I told her that after realising that she was drunk at her table, I thought it best to get her to bed in case anyone took advantage of her and that it was not something I was ever likely to do. We walked into the hotel arm in arm and Janice made me promise to keep the last dance for her on our final night of our Egyptian tour. It was a relaxed evening and almost everyone was dancing, except Eva, who had gone off with one of the men, much to my relief. Monica also invited me to dance with her and mentioned that she lived in Roundhay, Leeds, and had met someone on the previous singles' holiday. I could not resist teasing her.

"Surely as the leader, you are not allowed to snaffle one of the paying customers."

"Try telling him that since he was doing the snaffling and thinks it was worth every penny."

She had enjoyed the trip to Banana Island and was recommending that it should be offered on the tour as an option. At the end of our dance, I got another kiss on the cheek just as Dickie was dancing by and his eyebrows shot up with surprise. I knew my reputation would suffer as a result. After a jolly night with lots of toasts and having danced with most of the guests and our tour guide, Janice and I took to the floor for the last dance. I wondered if she thought we were still in the competition because she was holding me so tightly and wearing the semi-transparent white dress again. When the dance ended, she said she would like to sit on the river bench for our last evening in Egypt. We sat alongside the Nile looking up at the black velvet sky with its twinkling evening stars and she asked if I would come and visit her in Bridgend. I heard myself saying I would and was sure I had drunk too much. She put her arms around me and kissed me and as we stood to go up to the hotel, she pressed her cabin key into my hand.

During the long flight back home, Dickie told me that he would not be meeting Joan again after he learned that her thirty-year-old daughter had just divorced and come back to live with her. A few years earlier, he had been in love with a nurse and they were planning to get married until her eighteen-year-old daughter had destroyed the relationship by telling her mother appalling lies about him. He never learned what she had accused him of and was most hurt by the fact that his fiancée had believed her. Dickie and the daughter had not got on and since she had no job, or income, he was convinced that she had protected her lifestyle by making sure that her mother's marriage never took place. After this, he kept well away from women with daughters at home, who would see their mother taking a new husband as a threat, particularly if the mother was affluent.

I had really enjoyed the holiday, both for the wonderful sights I had seen and the fun and experience of being with my fellow single holidaymakers. I expected to find that Xmas and New Year would be pleasant, but just as quiet and uneventful as in every other year.

Chapter 6
New Year

After a very quiet Xmas with my daughter Abby and her boyfriend, when we were joined by Karen and her husband, I wondered about doing something special for New Year and noticed an advertisement for an overnight stay and New Year's Eve dinner dance at a Wetherby Hotel. I thought it was probably too late to make a booking, but when I rang, I was surprised to hear that after a cancellation, they still had one room available. I asked them to hold it for an hour and telephoned Jean at Haxby. After listening to the ring tone for some time and hoping she was in, Jean finally answered and apologised for the delay due to a persistent double-glazing salesman, who kept her at her front door and was still reluctant to leave so that she could answer her phone. Hearing her explanation, I responded.

"I thought you might have been chatting with Santa Claus about what you found in your Xmas stocking."

"The only thing I am likely to find in my stocking these days are holes, but I am always open to friendly visitors bearing gifts."

"Are you thinking of an old man driving a sleigh, or a tennis player driving a white BMW?"

"I don't really mind how he arrives as long as he can find my house."

"Well, I should have no trouble then and I am just wondering if you have made any plans for New Year's Eve?"

"As usual, Trudy has invited me around for drinks and another chance to watch that Scottish bagpiper screeching in the New Year perched on top of the battlements of Edinburgh castle, but with things as they are at present, the atmosphere in her house is just as fraught."

"How about spending it instead in a nice warm Wetherby hotel with dinner, followed by dancing the New Year in. Unfortunately, they only have one room left, but if we share a bed again, we can enjoy a late breakfast together in the morning?"

"Yet another invitation to another night away and risking my reputation and my pyjamas by sharing a bed with you. What a wonderful idea and of course, I would love to dance the New Year in with you and I might even manage a few cuddles as well. Where do I sign up?"

Just like me and many other retired and unattached people, it can be a lonely time of the year and we arranged to meet at the hotel, which was an easy drive for both of us.

I felt guilty about taking advantage of her whenever it suited me and used the phone call to suggest that I could drive over to Haxby to work on her repairs list whenever it suited her. She told me there was a play on at the York Theatre Royal which she would like to see and wondered if I would like to take her and do the repairs while I was there. It salved my conscience to agree to both and she said she would get the theatre tickets.

The play Jean wanted to see was very funny and well-acted. During the drinks' interval, Jean saw two local ladies staring at us as we stood together and told me they were terrible gossips. As she finished speaking, the ladies headed straight for us and told Jean that it was ages since they had last seen her and they wondered what she had been up to. They then looked closely at me as a possible culprit and paused until Jean introduced us. She told them we played tennis together sometimes and today I had joined her in coming to watch the play. The taller of the two then asked if I lived locally and I tried to make my answer as vague as possible.

"No. I live over in West Yorkshire, but I am now retired and I often come to York because I have friends here who play tennis."

Now it was the turn of the other lady to continue the interrogation. She smiled and seized on my comment that I was retired to find out a little more about the unknown man with Jean.

"And what did you do before you retired, Mr Hartley?"

Becoming irritated by their persistence and before I could stop myself, I told them:

"I was a practising gynaecologist."

Both ladies said "Oh" together and Jean turned her head away and struggled to keep a straight face and avoid laughing. The pair, having satisfied their curiosity and checked out the unknown man with their friend, told us it was time to return to their seats and walked off. Jean punched me on my arm and complained.

"You devil. Now they will be telling everyone that I am having it off with a gynaecologist."

"Sorry love. They made a beeline for you and were obviously determined to find out who you were with and it just slipped out. You could always tell them you are pregnant and I was just checking you out."

"Enough. You get worse. Now I will have to go along with it and admit that I know a tennis-playing gynaecologist, but when you said it, I watched the startled expression on their faces and I suppose it serves them right for being so nosey."

After the play ended, we drove back to Haxby and when we went to bed Jean again punched me on the shoulder and threatened me with wearing her tight-fitting swimsuit in bed unless I agreed to avoid embarrassing her again. Fortunately, neither of us was wearing pyjamas and naturally I agreed to her terms.

After breakfast the following morning, I put on my working clothes and started work on fixing sticking doors and adjusting cupboard hinges. Jean lived in a small bungalow with a detached garage, which had a badly painted and sagging door and loose frame. We drove to B&Q and Jean bought the paint, brushes and filler for me to fill the holes and do the painting. Since I was in my working clothes, I suggested that if we met any more of her friends, she could always tell them I was a tennis-playing decorator. My suggestion was ignored. After lunch together, I finished repairing the garage doors, sanding the woodwork and applying a good coat of paint to help them last a few more years. When I had cleaned up and changed, Jean made coffee and I told her about my concerns that I was taking advantage of her in suggesting occasional meetings and hoping that she would accept. Jean took my hand as she told me how she felt about us.

"Before we met in Cyprus, I had not been out with a man for some time and even when I did have a male escort, either they said very little or what they said was very boring. Some of them assumed that I was waiting for them to make love and their groping was clumsy and completely turned me off. I enjoy spending time with you and you always wait for me to give you encouragement before you take advantage. If I ever decide that I don't want to continue our meetings, or expect a more permanent arrangement, I will tell you so. Until then, I live in Haxby and you live near Leeds and I see no reason why we should not meet whenever we want."

I had my answer and I was relieved to be able to meet up with Jean from time to time. The days seem to fly when you are busy, retired and enjoying life and Jean and I were soon meeting up for our stay over the New Year at Wetherby. The hotel room was adequate, but just like most major hotel groups everywhere, it was completely soulless. The New Year's Eve dinner was average and we were sharing a table with a married couple from Garforth, who introduced themselves as Betty and Ken. Betty asked where we lived and unfortunately Jean and I both answered at the same time and gave different towns. A strange look came over Betty's face and there was no further conversation with our fellow guests. Talking about this reaction later with Jean, we decided that Betty had strong views about avoiding unmarried couples living in sin. We also agreed that our relationship was definitely not living in sin, at least not for most of the time. The music was played by a DJ and Jean laughed when I asked her to dance with a fallen man. I enjoyed the waltz and quickstep dances which were fitted in with the usual stand and shake current dance style. We had to form a chain and do the conga dance around the ballroom and out into the foyer, but even seniors can make fools of themselves when it suits them. As the evening ended with us all joining arms and singing Auld Lang Syne, we agreed that it had been a really special night, which was far better than sitting at home watching our televisions and hitting the gin bottle. After breakfast on the first day of the New Year, I saw Jean to her car and she told me the courts at her club would soon be finished and she was looking forward to playing with me again. I liked the way Jean invited me to see her, but with no pressure and always with a quick kiss on the cheek.

While Dickie and I were in Egypt, Jean and Trudy had been on a short break in Blackpool and sent me a naughty postcard, fortunately hidden in an envelope. I thought they were now out of print, but obviously Jean had put away a small supply to send to friends and pyjama haters. Her message said that in bracing Blackpool, they had almost been swept off the promenade by the gale force winds and missed the presence of two able-bodied men, conspicuous by their absence. Their next short break was to be in Llandudno and could we recommend two suitable men willing to be their escorts. The card was amongst a pile of mail behind my door when I returned from Egypt and after reading it and then contacting Jean about New Year, it had slipped my mind. Surprisingly Jean had not mentioned the invitation during our stay at Weatherby, probably because she thought we were not interested. I would have to talk to Dickie about suitable dates, since I was sure that he would not want to miss a weekend with Trudy. Over lunch at The Yorkshireman, we chose dates and I rang Jean to ask if these were convenient and apologised for my late response. She told me she was not surprised with my hectic life style but promised to come back to me after checking with Trudy. Within minutes, I had my answer and we would be taking the girls for our first get-together since the Cyprus holiday. I decided to pack my warmest clothes for walks along the promenade.

We met the two girls at Leeds Railway Station and fortunately the car had a big boot, since the two cases the girls carried were very bulky and heavy. It seemed incredible that they needed so much luggage for just a two-night stay. Jean sat in the front and Dickie and Trudy in the back. The sun was shining and the car heater kept us warm as we made our way to the North Wales coast. It was a pleasant drive in charming company and Dickie told the girls that I had taken yoga classes. I did not mention being the only man and that I would be taking no more lessons. When asked about the course I simply told them I had enjoyed myself and it was very good for the body, but having tried it I thought my tennis and golf gave me quite enough exercise. Jean gave me a quizzical look and would probably want to know more when we were alone but kept silent in the car. Both girls wanted to hear about our holiday in Egypt and I left it to Dickie to describe the sights, the beggars and my organised river cruise. He kept my performance with the belly dancer until last and as they were still laughing, told them how I won the dance competition. He did not tell them we had been on a singles' holiday. Jean complained that my triumph had not been recorded on camera, but at least I was able to show them our photograph with the camels behind us. After stopping on the way to have a light lunch, we arrived around 3 pm. We were booked in at a hotel right in the middle of the sea front esplanade and our bedroom window gave us a clear view of the angry grey waves rushing towards the beach below.

Trudy wanted to see the Great Orme, but the late afternoon was the wrong time to enjoy the magnificent views and we walked along the pier instead. As we stood together at the pier end, the wind was so strong that it was actually pushing us backwards. Trudy amazed us by saying she fancied an ice cream. We shuddered at the thought as we battled our way back down the pier in the powerful winds. It was a relief to reach the shelter of the town centre buildings and we found a café selling coffee and ice cream. Trudy enjoyed her cold treat as we enjoyed our hot coffee. Dickie jokingly asked if she was pregnant and Trudy surprised us with a very loud denial that hell would freeze over first. I thought Trudy's high spirits were suspicious and that she might be over compensating for problems of some sort.

Over dinner, we drank two bottles of wine and Trudy accounted for more than her share, which confirmed my view that there was something wrong. We joined in the evening bingo competition and Trudy had a full house and won £20. After collecting her money, she told us.

"You know what they say about being lucky with money and unlucky in love; well, that's me."

We looked at her in surprise but were not told what the problem was before the evening entertainment began. A woman with heavy makeup and wearing a dress a size too small for her, which forced her flesh to bulge out in certain areas, began singing a selection of popular songs. I suspected that her age was well over fifty, but she had a strong, clear voice and I enjoyed her performance. The dancing began afterwards and I danced with Jean first and then Trudy. As we were dancing together, I asked Trudy if she was worried about anything and after a long pause, she told me that it was just arguments at home with her useless husband. By eleven o'clock, we were ready for bed and when I warned Dickie that there would be no more room swapping, he looked horrified. As soon as we were in bed, Jean wrapped herself around me and demanded to be told what had gone wrong at my yoga classes. I told her about being grabbed and kissed in the apartment of my yoga tutor and Jean laughed before sympathising with me.

"Oh, how awful that must have been for you after walking into her lion's den. You are going to have to take a much stronger approach with these designing females who keep assaulting you, or you will to end up as someone's husband."

Then it was my turn to ask questions about her friend.

"What is worrying Trudy? Her high spirits don't fool me and I feel sure she is hiding some sort of problem, perhaps with her husband."

"Yes, her husband is the problem. He is unhappy about having to sleep in a separate bedroom and wants a divorce so that he can live with a woman he met in France. The children are grown up and he wants to sell the house and give her a half share. He earns good money driving and she suspects he has been planning this for a while and has been putting cash away to keep it from her in the divorce. Trudy has no money of her own and her part-time job pays very little, but it got her out of the house. The divorce will leave her homeless."

"Well, Jean, we will just have to put our heads together and find ways of helping her to make sure she gets all that she is entitled to. She deserves it after putting up with this man for so long and bearing his children. At the very least, she is entitled to half the house."

"I told her you would know what she should do. You are good."

I turned around to face her in the bed and tried to prove that I had other talents.

When I woke up the following morning, I could hear a strange tapping noise and it seemed to be coming from the window, which seemed odd since we were on the second floor. When I got up and drew the curtains, I saw an enormous seagull perched on the sill and looking at me, presumably hoping to be fed. I banged the glass a couple of times and it flew away, but the noise had wakened Jean. She wanted to know why I was standing stark naked at the window and accused me of being a second-floor flasher. I jumped back in bed and said it was too early to get up and I was cold and needed warming up.

As we were dressing, I asked whether Trudy was thinking of moving in with Dickie. Jean told me not to say anything to Dickie about Trudy facing the prospect of losing the house and only mention the divorce. If Dickie cared enough for her, he might suggest that Trudy moved in with him, but she would not want him to do this because he felt sorry for her. At her age, losing her man and home was bad enough without risking another bad relationship with a new man.

During breakfast, nothing was said about Trudy's domestic problems and I carefully avoided the subject. After breakfast, we drove to the top of the Great Orme and the wind was so strong that I had difficulty opening the car doors. We had come to look at the view and in spite of the stormy weather, walked around the cliff top to look down on the foaming grey sea as we were rocked on our feet by the force of the wind. It had been many years since I last visited the Great Orme and I suggested we go inside out of the wind and have coffee or ice creams. I told them how I had once called to collect an outstanding debt to my company when the building was owned by an ex-champion boxer. The manageress told me that she would have to get the cheque signed by the owner, who was resting. I told her that she had given the same excuse on my last visit and if the account was not settled that day, the matter would go to court. She then led me through the building and opened the door for me to speak with the owner. The man was lying stark naked on a bed with the biggest erection I am ever likely to see. I explained my need for his signature and stood by the bed with my eyes rigidly focused on his face as he signed and returned the cheque to me. Trudy giggled and asked if it was really that big and I replied.

"It was enormous and now I think of the Great Orme as the Great Horn."

Trudy laughed at this and at least my true story had brought a little humour into the morning. I suggested driving to the Tweedmill Shopping Outlet, where there was free parking and we could stroll around the shops under cover and perhaps stay for lunch. It was only a half hour drive and after parking, we split up so that the girls could browse the lady's outlets, while Dickie and I visited the remaining shops. Dickie bought a sweater and I bought shoes at a Pavers store. We joined up for lunch and both girls were carrying bulky packages and seemed to have enjoyed themselves. It was warm and dry inside the outlet and we stayed for the afternoon and visited every area. January can be a bad month for weather, but at least there was no snow and rain to dampen our spirits. I asked Dickie if he knew about Trudy being divorced and he said he knew but did not suggest that he would be taking advantage by having a closer relationship with her. He had been living on his own for many years and perhaps he was now too entrenched in his lifestyle to change his ways. He also had bad memories of his previous marriage and would not want a repeat. He really enjoyed Trudy's company and I assumed she had cured his sex problem, but only he would know if his feelings for her were strong enough to share his life with her.

Dinner that evening was noticeably quiet and no mention was made of the divorce. Trudy and Dickie seemed to be more affectionate to each other and perhaps it was best to let whatever was happening between them take its course. After the evening entertainment ended, they went off to bed and Jean and I sat drinking coffee in the lounge. Her husband had told Trudy that he would give her half the money from the house sale, but that would only allow her to buy half a house or something to that value. I suggested that she should go to a solicitor who specialised in divorce cases to make sure that she received everything she was entitled to. Jean promised she would keep me informed so that I could advise Trudy as things progressed. Trudy had two daughters who were married and had young children but no room to accommodate their mother after the house was sold.

We had booked only two nights, since Trudy would be at work on Monday morning. During the drive back to Yorkshire, there was very little conversation, which allowed me to play soft music to try to ease the tension. At least I enjoyed it, but my passengers probably failed to hear it as they sat quietly and dwelt on their own problems.

Chapter 7
Thailand

Dickie was not his usual boisterous self for days after our weekend in Llandudno and I guessed that he was trying to decide whether he should move his relationship with Trudy to a more permanent basis. I knew that he had strong feelings for her and she always made him laugh and brighten up. He had always assured me that he had the perfect lifestyle, meeting lots of new ladies and going whenever and wherever he pleased. He would have married the nurse who was told lies about him by her daughter and he was upset when two years later he learned from a friend that she was now married to someone else after her daughter had left home. A vindictive daughter had destroyed what I expected would have been a good second marriage for him. Divorce proceedings began for Trudy, but they would go on for some time and I wondered if a holiday in the sun would lighten Dickie's mood. It was only six weeks since we had returned from Egypt, but now that we were retired, there was no limit on the number of holidays we took and I really enjoyed hot sunshine and warm sea. I hurried through the cold wind to meet Dickie and sit at our usual table before the roaring wood fire in our local pub. I put a brochure showing details of the Phuket and Pattaya, Thailand holiday in his hands. Some five years previously I had holidayed in Bangkok and Chiang Mai and was fascinated by the people and country.

It was a late booking bargain with 10% discount and if Dickie was not interested, I might drive down to Bridgend to stay with Janice, but at this time of the year South Wales might be just as cold and windy as North Wales. Dickie put the brochure down on the bar table and smiled at me.

"Nice one, my friend. Looks good, good price and at least it will be warm and you can get your shorts on. They also do cheap suits there and mine are getting a bit worn. You might get lucky again and meet more of your lady boys."

We had ten days to get ready and the injections for the Egyptian holiday would still hold good. The currency was the Thai baht, but friends had suggested we take dollars since it would be cheaper to buy bahts when we arrived, but only if they were needed. Flights, local transport and half board accommodation were covered and we would also be able to use our credit cards. It should be warmer when we returned, the tennis courts could be opening and golf courses would have dried out ready for another English spring. As a teenager, I always felt sorry for retired people because of their restricted lifestyles and limited activities. Now that people are living longer and keeping fitter as they grow older, they are able to lead more energetic lives and enjoy many sporting activities. Dickie and I were more adventurous and enjoying a much more varied and exciting time than we ever had when we were teenagers. Back then we were always mindful that unprotected physical contact with a girl could result in an unwelcome pregnancy and a forced teenage marriage. Senior citizens are now able to decide if and with whom they are prepared to sleep, but without the possibility of unwanted pregnancy. However, the danger of infection through having multiple partners still exists and is best avoided by using a condom.

Our flight from Manchester landed at Dubai and we spent some time walking the length of the magnificent terminal with its enormous range of shops and restaurants, which would put the average UK shopping centre to shame. There were palm trees lining the walkways and escalators to allow passengers to access the various shopping levels. Knowing that we would be returning to the terminal on our flight back from Pattaya, I suggested that we resist the low prices and leave our purchases until we were homeward bound. Our next flight was to the island of Phuket and after eighteen hours travelling time in total, we reached our first holiday location. The hotel was near Cape Panwa in the south of the island and it had its own beach and a small pier. Looking at the gorgeous white sand, blue sea and palm trees surrounding the beach swimming area, I thought that even if we spent the entire time there it would still be a dream holiday. We were both tired after the long flights and hours spent at Dubai before changing planes for Phuket. We went to bed and woke in time to have lunch and then spent the afternoon at the hotel beach.

There was a grand pagoda style building where we were given large towels and a young man walked with us along the beach to place sun loungers on the sand, with a canopy to shield us from the hot sun. A waiter then came to serve us and we ordered cold drinks. We were being pampered and it was a very enjoyable experience. Leaving Dickie to relax, I swam out to the pier and found the sea warm and full of fish. Knowing that the Andaman Sea was ideal for swimming, I had brought a snorkel and found myself surrounded by fish of all shapes and colours. As I swam amongst them, I could feel them brush against me and it was fascinating to watch entire shoals of fish turn and twist as one. Either their reactions were incredible, or they were somehow able to communicate with each other.

When I swam back to the beach, a bronzed young woman was kneeling beside Dickie and massaging his chest. Wearing a tight-fitting bra and shorts, her arms and legs rippled with muscle and under her vigorous pummelling, Dickie's spare flesh was being pushed from side to side. Seeing me standing beside him with seawater dripping onto his towel, he insisted that I should be next for the treatment to loosen me up after the long flight and my swim.

"You have to give this a try. I can feel myself glowing all over and relaxing after all that travelling. You didn't tell me it was going to take most of a day to get here."

Satisfied that my swim had already made up for the hours spent on my bottom during the flights, I turned down his suggestion and left him in the hands of his muscular lady. I wanted to find out what other facilities were on offer at the hotel. The pagoda housed a large restaurant and a tourist booking office with a smiling young woman sitting at her desk, who was anxious to tell me all about the wonderful adventures she could arrange. We could be taken to islands where we could shoot, enjoy quad bike rides through the jungle, snorkel or scuba dive to coral reefs, visit a casino or go to a show with elephants and aerial acrobats. Perhaps there would not be enough time to try them all, but I hoped to persuade Dickie to try most of them. As I was speaking to the young woman, I heard a loud man's voice behind me say that he would like to try the quad bikes and then Artie and Glenda introduced themselves. They were on holiday from Melbourne in Australia and had just flown from Bangkok. They were a lively pair and I invited them to have their sun lounger parked alongside ours on the beach and introduced them to Dickie, after waking him after his strenuous pummelling by Miss Muscles. Artie owned a building business and his wife worked in his office. It was their first holiday for ten years and their son was looking after the business while they were away. Glenda had relatives in Kent and Artie had a brother in Essex and they planned to visit the UK when they retired in five years' time. We arranged to meet them for dinner in the hotel and enjoy the evening entertainment together.

The hotel was running a special buffet and barbecue for the evening. Guests could help themselves to the indoor buffet selection of cooked meat and fish dishes, or choose tiger prawns, or meat on skewers and cook them on the outdoor barbecue. The food was delicious and we added two bottles of wine and were in fine form when the curtains at the far end of the restaurant opened and six magnificent dancers paraded on stage. They were stunningly attractive, with their slim figures and beautiful faces. All were wearing short skirts to show off their long and shapely legs. After they finished their act, a single dancer came on stage wearing a loose-fitting black net top, which gave us a clear view of her well-shaped breasts. She did a slow dance to a vocal recording of *Diamonds Are a Girl's Best Friend* and made sure that we all saw her breasts move from side to side in time with the music. Artie had drunk much of the wine and could not take his eyes off her. Suddenly, as the music faded, he spoke out in a loud voice:

"I know it's a bloody fellah, but he must have tucked his dick up—"

Glenda grabbed her husband and stopped him from telling everyone the exact location. Fortunately, the dancer either did not hear or decided not to react to Artie's claim. Some UK guests at the next table who did hear Artie began laughing and told us that the lady boys used hormone creams to allow them to grow breasts. Not to be silenced, Artie carried on with his views.

"That hormone cream must be pretty dinkum to grow breasts like those, but no way is it going to dissolve dicks as well."

The group alongside us couldn't stop laughing and joined us on the terrace for coffee at the close of the performance. I guessed that the lady boys could understand English because when she, or he was leaving, the performer wearing the see-through net top pursed his lips in a mock kiss for Artie, who snorted his disapproval. Over coffee, we arranged with Artie to go shooting the next morning and would be back just after lunch in time to change to see the elephant show. We were all glad to make our way to our rooms to finish making up for missed sleep during our long journeys. Next morning, we were waiting with other guests for a boat to take us out to one of the many islands off the coast. We were told to wear shorts and sandals because we would have to wade out to the boat, since the tide would be out.

The boat held six guests and two crewmembers and it was powered by a large motor at the end of a long shaft operating a propeller. The crewman moved the motor and shaft together to steer the boat and our journey took forty minutes. Once again, we had to wade through the water to get ashore and were then taken to the shooting ground. There were ten targets set up in a line facing each aiming point where we chose weapons. My guess was that the range was around twenty-five yards long. I chose a Kalashnikov rifle and Dickie picked up a Glock automatic handgun. Each was loaded with ten rounds and I watched Dickie take aim and empty his gun as he hit three of the targets. That was pretty good shooting with a handgun at that range. I lined up the sights and fired my first shot, which hit the target centre and I was surprised that the sights were correctly set and it was firing true. Taking my time, I hit eight more targets and then Dickie slapped me on the shoulder and called me Buffalo Bill. I missed with my tenth shot after his interruption but was very impressed with the gun and understood why it was so popular worldwide. Artie had also chosen a Kalashnikov rifle and had no trouble putting all of his ten rounds in the targets. He explained that he often went shooting dingo dogs with a farming friend who wanted to protect his stock from them. We were back in good time to get changed and around thirty guests boarded a coach to take us to the elephant show.

Driving north, we were surprised to see a large fishing trawler lying at the side of the road and our guide told us it had been swept ashore by the tsunami the previous year. The sea was at least a quarter of a mile away and to move a boat of that size it must have been a giant wave. When we reached the entertainment centre, we drove through an impressive stone arch before walking across the coach park to watch a group of elephants being hosed down. A stall was selling bananas in paper bags to feed the elephants and I bought a bag and walked over to stand watching the giant animals. I intended to feed them one banana at a time, but suddenly a long trunk reached down over my shoulder and snatched my bag full of bananas, which then disappeared up into the mouth of a very large elephant standing immediately behind me. It must have moved there as I was watching the others and I backed away from the giant animal as fast as I could to avoid being tossed aside by its trunk or stamped on by its enormous feet. Later, our group was seated in a theatre with the front half level and the rear half raised to give a good view of the performance arena. The two halves were divided by a wide walkway and we were in the raised half immediately alongside the walkway.

The curtains opened and the arena was empty apart from a set of goalposts on the left. A young man appeared leading an elephant which was wearing a football cap, jersey and an enormous pair of shorts. The elephant then stood as goalkeeper between the posts as another elephant entered, pushing a football forward with its trunk. After moving the ball around with its trunk for a minute or two, it suddenly flicked the ball at the goal. The goalkeeper elephant swept it aside with its own trunk and then began swaying from left to right in triumph. The ball was returned to the striker elephant, which casually moved it around again with its trunk before craftily kicking it at the goal with its back foot and scoring. Now the striker elephant swayed in triumph and the audience roared with laughter. Two large chart pads on easels were set up and a paintbrush was placed in the trunk of each elephant. After the football act, we were ready for anything, but were again amazed to see each elephant paint a scene with palm trees around a sandy beach. The keepers passed different coloured brushes for the elephants to hold in their trunks. The paintings were then offered for sale and I had to restrain Dickie.

"If you tell our friends that it was painted by an elephant you are never going to convince them, unless you can get it signed."

Dickie ignored my humour but took my advice. Artie jumped up and was one of the first to buy a painting and when he returned, I suggested he ask the keeper to have the elephant sign it by putting its footprint on the back. He was on his way back up to the stage before Glenda could stop him. Hearing Artie's request, the keeper looked a little surprised but nodded his head and smeared some cream on the elephant's foot, then lowered it on to the back of the painting. Artie returned in triumph waving his authenticated painting with a full-size elephant footprint filling the back. Glenda and I locked eyes in amazement. My fun suggestion had produced a great souvenir. Dickie congratulated me and I kept my silence and assumed the unintended credit for my suggestion. Speaking with Glenda in the coach as we drove back to the hotel, she told me she would have the painting framed. I suggested she put it between two sheets of clear glass so that both sides were exposed for admirers in Australia to see and be impressed. I thought the elephant's footprint was far better than the crude painting on the front.

The curtains re-opened and a man on a one-wheeled cycle with a three feet high seat began riding around the stage, before being joined by a small monkey riding a smaller two-wheeled cycle. In Thailand, monkeys are sent to the top of coconut palms to shake off loose coconuts to prevent them falling on unsuspecting tourists some fifty feet below. The monkeys are on long chains to be sure they return after their climb and are then moved to other coconut palms. The curtains closed and the lights dimmed and a pair of high wire acrobats flew over the audience with flashing lights on their feet. This was followed by a trapeze artist outlined by more flashing lights against a dark background. Next, as we looked up, we could see a dozen figures flying over us surrounded by flashing laser beams and the sound of loud music. The darkness hid the wires supporting them and made the effect very dramatic. The show ended, but we were told to remain in our seats to watch as fifteen large elephants began to parade along the walkway in front of us, each holding the tail of the elephant in front. After a pause, three baby elephants passed before us and the crowd were laughing and clapping simultaneously. It had been a great show and an incredible first full day for us.

Next morning, Dickie and I with Glenda and Artie were waiting for the mini coach to take us to the quad bike centre. Glenda was not going to ride but wanted to keep an eye on Artie after I told him that the instructors were probably all lady boys. The journey took an hour and we then had to sign forms assuming responsibility for any accidents we might have on the bikes, before strapping on our helmets and goggles. After a short session on our machines at the training ground, a group of six bold riders rode out behind our instructor. He had a shaven head and was shirtless to show his muscular torso. Glenda glared at me as she told Artie that he was clearly not a lady boy. A track took us around the administration centre and through a shallow stream with high sandy sides to train us in controlling our machine. I was next to the leader, followed by Dickie and then Artie and the remaining riders. We drove at speed through the stream to create a bow wave around us and our photographs were taken and could be purchased as souvenirs. A narrow track led into the jungle and it was uneven and pitted with tree roots and stones, which tilted the bike from side to side. It had to be controlled with a firm grip on the handles, but fortunately there were no mishaps. Next the leader took us down an incline and shouted, "Water ahead." As we approached, I could see that we were driving down into a valley bottom with a stream to cross. I turned and shouted to Dickie and Artie to accelerate as soon as the bike reached the stream. I accelerated as my front wheel reached the water, which was roughly two feet deep and the power drove the bike through and up the other side of the bank. My two friends followed and did the same, but the rider behind them did not and got stuck in the middle of the water and blocked the trail. We carried on up the slope and stopped behind the leader, who used his telephone to speak to a helper standing watch at the crossing. It was his responsibility to extract waterlogged riders who regularly stalled quadbikes in the stream. We drove on and crossed over a sandy beach, just skirting the waves as we dodged past broken palm tree trunks caused by the tsunami. We returned to Glenda in triumph and all bought dramatic photos showing intrepid riders on quadbikes surging through a wave of water and foam.

At dinner that evening, we were entertained by Thai girls in traditional ankle length sarongs, who danced on bare feet and used their hands and arms to express the message of the songs. Glenda assured Artie that they were genuine ladies and gave me a hard look as she spoke, which ensured my silence. The next day, we were parting company since Dickie and I were off to Phi Phi Island to snorkel over the coral reef and Glenda and Artie were visiting the Wat Chalong Temple. We visited Phuket Town and Patong and spent our last two days lazing on the beach and soaking up the sun. When we said goodbye to Glenda and Artie, we exchanged addresses and urged the Australians to come and visit us on their retirement vacation to the UK. Similarly, we were offered hospitality if we visited Melbourne. I knew I would not be able to cope with the two-day flight to Australia by going direct, but perhaps by breaking both journeys at Singapore, it would be bearable. Perhaps I could also visit my son Michael. Phuket is a place I would be happy to return to at any time and Singapore is my favourite city.

Our second half of the holiday was at Pattaya and we first flew to Bangkok and stayed one night in a luxurious hotel near the Chao Phraya River in the city centre. Spiced food has a cleansing effect on me and after dinner when we reached our hotel room I made straight for the toilet. When I flushed it, the bowl failed to empty and I was startled to watch the water almost reach the top. There was a blockage, but without any means of clearing it, despite my embarrassment, I was forced to ring reception. Fortunately, it was a young man who arrived with whatever was needed to solve the problem. I was more embarrassed having him work through my mess, but he told me that it often happened because the system was overloaded. I wondered how much of the city sewage ended up in the river.

After dinner, we walked around the area with its brightly lit stalls along the roadsides selling a wide range of food, clothes, watches, electronic ware and even pepper sprays. The traffic was noisy and spewing out thick smoke fumes from noisy engines, which is probably why many pedestrians were wearing masks over their mouths. Tuktuks were everywhere as they ferried passengers around the city. They have a motorcycle front and a wide rear on two wheels which can carry two passengers side by side. I told Dickie I could taste the air as we walked along the streets and we both wanted to get away from the fumes. After hurrying back to the hotel, I saw a sign in reception reading 'Swimming Pool, floor twenty-three' and we went to the top floor to investigate. It was large and spotlessly clean on the surrounding paved area. It was also floodlit and surrounded by a high rail and wire barrier, which allowed viewing of the city lights below without risking life. We went to our room to change into our swim trunks and returned. The air seemed clear and was pleasantly warm and without flies, which fortunately had insufficient wing power to make it to this height. There were only two other swimmers in the pool and they soon left so that we had this wonderful area to ourselves. A waiter came and we ordered cold drinks before sitting alongside the water under a sky full of stars and drinking our Tiger beer. It was a wonderful way to spend our only night in Bangkok. After breakfast next day, we boarded our coach for the long journey south to Pattaya.

The journey took hours and when we finally reached our hotel in Pattaya, we were stiff and sweaty. After lunch, we both wanted to relax in the sun and found a shaded corner where we could stretch out and enjoy our cold drinks. The hotel was at the edge of a long sandy beach, but two young Australians at the next table advised us to swim in the pool and avoid the sea. Jack and Liam were newly qualified Australian doctors having a well-earned holiday and told us that Bangkok was north of us and the sea current could carry all sorts of nasty things south. I told them about Artie and Glenda, and they said Thailand was very popular with Australians. I thought the countries were similar except that there were no crocodiles in Thailand. According to Jack, the Thai people had probably eaten them, since they also ate fried insects, ants' eggs, tadpoles, bamboo worms and monkeys. They intended to visit the Walking Street after dinner and invited us to join them. I kicked Dickie's leg and said we wanted to stay in the hotel to recover from our bus journey. When we were alone, I explained that if the Walking Street lived up to its reputation, I would prefer to visit it without two young macho Australians along to set the pace. We believed that by visiting the Walking Street during the day we would be safer than doing so at night and went into town by Tuktuk after breakfast. The street was the usual mix of bars, restaurants, clubs and souvenir shops and there were quite a few people exploring like us. I was following Dickie and looking inside the shops as I walked along when he suddenly disappeared. I walked on and found my arm gripped as I was pulled inside a bar by two scantily dressed but powerful ladies. At least I assumed they were ladies, but in Thailand, who knows? Inside the gloomy room, I found Dickie sitting at a table with a drink in his hand, which he waved at me and told me to sit down in the booth beside him. I did and a drink was quickly put in front of me on the table.

I had heard of pole dancers and thought they were ladies dancing around some sort of scaled down maypole. The three ladies on stage were dressed only in skimpy loincloths, at least I think they were wearing something, but in the darkened room and with their revolving bodies bathed in the bright spotlight beam I could not be sure. All three looked at us as they pressed their bodies tightly against a pole held between their legs and I told Dickie they might also be lady boys, but he was not convinced. I watched as they moved suggestively up and down and wondered if the pole was wooden or metal. With wood, the girls risked serious harm from splinters, so the poles were probably metal and their bodies were oiled. An older lady suddenly appeared and sat down beside me and told me her name, which sounded like Fah. She asked for my name and where I lived and then began massaging my back with very strong hands. There was also a lady alongside Dickie and I guessed that he was getting the same treatment. We were trapped, but I hesitated about being rude or forceful, knowing they were only trying to earn a living. Just as I decided what to do, my lady put her arm around my neck and asked if I wanted to go upstairs. I took out two five-dollar bills and gave one to my lady and slipped the other under my untouched drink, telling Dickie to do the same. I had to push hard to move the woman sideways to make room and then jumped up and rushed for the door. Dickie was right behind me and we walked quickly towards the busy town centre, not stopping until we were safely inside a shopping mall.

We had walked around most of the mall by lunchtime and decided to eat in a large restaurant with a spectacular water feature in the middle. It had a range of fountains surrounding a large pool with brightly coloured fish swimming around.

Dickie chose fried chicken and I opted for a chicken salad. Since it was only a mile walk back to our hotel, we decided to get some exercise but took a wide detour as we avoided the Walking Street. We went for a swim in the hotel pool and were resting alongside when I knew that I had to race to the toilet. For the next day and a half, I refused to move more than five yards from our bathroom and used tablets to fight off the infection. Town centre restaurants washed salads in river or local water which had no effect on Thai nationals but could leave unsuspecting tourists stranded near toilets. When I recovered, I found my shorts kept slipping down and I had to wear a belt to keep them in place. On our last day, we visited Wat Phra Yai Temple with its fifty feet tall golden Buddha. We were told to wear long trousers because of the dress code and when we reached the temple, we were given helmets to wear because construction work was still in progress. Set alongside the white sand of the Andaman Sea with its numerous spires and high central tower, the temple is magnificent. Made entirely of teak wood, it has incredible and intricate carving with very erotic life size figures and pillars created by the talented local craftsmen. I wanted to walk back to our hotel, but Dickie thought the afternoon heat would be a problem and once again we ended up in the back of a Tuktuk. Our last swim in the hotel pool and the cold drinks afterwards put us in mellow mood and we talked through our frantic escape from the ladies in the Walking Street club. We agreed that we were cowards, but we might have escaped from a very expensive and embarrassing situation. Throughout our holiday, we found the Thai people were always smiling and happy and anxious to do their best to ensure that visiting tourists enjoyed their holiday. We certainly did.

On the flight home, Dickie was more relaxed and I asked whether he had reached any decisions about his relationship with Trudy. He surprised me by saying that when the divorce was finalised or if Trudy became homeless, he would welcome her to his home and perhaps if all went well, he would marry her. I was really pleased for him and for Trudy even though I would be losing my travelling companion. He asked me to say nothing to Jean or Trudy until he found the right moment to talk it over and be sure that Trudy wanted to move in with him. When he dozed off, it occurred to me that Jean would also be losing her travelling companion and this could alter the current arrangement between us. I fell asleep before reaching any conclusion about how Jean might react and the effect on my newly established lifestyle. We travelled back from the airport by taxi and as it approached Fairfields estate, I looked at the overgrown patch of land at the entrance and thought what a bad impression visitors would have on seeing it for the first time. Arriving at my house, I had to push hard on the front door to move the bundle of mail which had accumulated during the holiday. I wondered how many trees had been chopped down to produce the paper for the letters and pamphlets offering me new windows, insurance cover, local groceries, or takeaway meals.

Chapter 8
Neighbourhood Watch

Amongst my mail was a letter from Janice telling me that she was having a new kitchen fitted and would I like to come and cut the tape and let her cook a meal for me. We had not exchanged telephone numbers after the holiday, but she put her number on her letter. I thought I would telephone her after settling in following the holiday to Thailand. It was a five-hour drive to Bridgend, which was over two hundred and fifty miles away, but it was spring and there were places I would like to visit near Janice. Dickie had told me he would be arranging to meet Trudy and I wanted to keep out of his way as he was sorting out his love life.

I was pleased to also find in my mail an invitation to a meeting at The Yorkshireman to discuss setting up a neighbourhood watch in the area. I was not aware of any burglaries, or muggings locally, but was conscious of my preoccupation with my own affairs and thought it was time to get involved with my neighbours. Just before flying off to Thailand, I used my battery charger to help my jogger neighbour Helen with her flat car battery, which was my first real local involvement since moving in to my house six months previously. I was washing my car and heard the familiar sounds of a flat battery abortive start up and naturally walked over to offer my help. The next day, she came around to my house with a cake she had baked and I invited her in for coffee and a chat. Helen was a retired nurse and bought her house when it was first built some two years previously. She liked the way I had partly flagged my front garden to avoid having a lawn to cut and wanted to do the same in her own. I promised to write out a step-by-step guide for her and felt guilty that it had slipped my mind. The pub landlord was holding a neighbourhood watch meeting at The Yorkshireman the next night and she would probably be there, so I would have to get the notes for her garden done beforehand. After shopping for groceries and returning to cook an evening meal, I decided to walk to the pub. There was no sign of Dickie and I was sitting alone with my drink when Helen appeared and asked if she could join me. As she sat at my table she asked about the holiday.

"The brown arms and face show that you were in the sun wherever you were on holiday."

I rubbed my forehead and felt the dry skin, which told me it would not be long before the tan was replaced by new white skin, unless we had a burst of spring sunshine to top it up.

"I was with my friend Dickie in Thailand and spent as much time as I could in the sea, or the shade, but just walking around you get caught by the hot sun."

I told her about the elephants and the lady boys and asked about her career as a nurse. Helen explained that she had trained as a midwife and ended up in a senior position. Her career meant everything to her and she had never married. I asked her about the overgrown patch of land near the entrance to our housing development, which I saw as an eyesore. Helen told me that initially it was cultivated and planted with shrubs and roses, but after all the houses were sold, the builders lost interest and it gradually filled with weeds and rubbish.

"Why are you so interested in that patch of land, Tom, it isn't big enough to build a house on?"

I explained that on the Fairfield development each household seemed to keep to itself and I was wondering if it was possible to create community spirit by encouraging residents to get involved together on some sort of project. The neighbourhood watch meeting might be the best place to begin. I had heard about residents elsewhere working together to build gardens which enhanced their area, provided healthy outdoor exercise and led to other joint activities. I wanted to suggest that we formed a garden club to convert the eyesore to an area to be proud of as well as forming a neighbourhood watch team. Looking at the pub clock, I was surprised that we had been chatting for almost two hours. I remembered going to the bar for more drinks and Helen had also bought a round. The jet lag and drinks were beginning to put pressure on my eyelids and I would be embarrassed if I began yawning whilst in conversation with Helen. I told her I needed to put my soiled holiday clothes in my washing machine and it was time for me to leave. When I mentioned this to Helen, she burst out laughing and asked which washing powder I could recommend. Her house was close to mine and we walked back together and agreed to be at the watch meeting the next night.

The landlord of The Yorkshireman pub was Rodney James and he and some regular customers were organising the watch meeting, which was being held in the pub's function room. It was used for wedding receptions, Rotary meetings, birthday parties and the occasional funeral wake. Rod had told me he was expecting forty people and when I arrived the room was already filled with locals. Rod opened the meeting and introduced the first speaker who told us about avoiding burglaries by fitting five lever locks on doors, movement activated floodlights and locking windows. A second speaker warned us about responding to phone calls supposedly from our bank, or the police, which could trick us into giving our bank details, or even handing over cash or valuable possessions to a convincing caller, ostensibly for safe-keeping.

The last speaker was from an established neighbourhood watch team who explained how crime had reduced after the members followed advice on security measures and took note of suspicious visitors in the area. It was decided to set up a scheme in Fairfields with Rod as the prime coordinator. He then introduced me and told the audience I had a proposal.

I explained how depressing it was to enter the Fairfields estate past an ugly, overgrown and rubbish filled plot, which must give visitors a poor impression of the area. Working together we could clear and plant the plot by forming a garden club. Those who were retired and those with jobs could all get involved to plan, build and maintain a garden for all to enjoy by giving some time to the work. Surprisingly, after asking for a show of hands, twenty people wanted to become involved and I asked them to join me after the meeting. Helen was amongst the group and I asked her if she would take names and telephone or e-mail addresses to make contact and arrange the first meeting. After the meeting closed, it was still only nine o'clock and Helen offered to buy me a drink.

"I was going to buy drinks last night, but could see you were struggling to keep your eyes open. We were chatting away and I didn't think I was boring you and put it down to jet lag, so it must be my turn to buy the drinks tonight."

As we were sitting together in the bar, I gave her my action plan for her front garden but suggested she should wait until our garden group began working on the plot at the estate entrance. We might need her surplus soil and could possibly supply hardcore for laying her flagstones. Helen told me that she had a friend in Manchester who had been in her nurses training programme and they had become very close. After qualifying, her friend got married and Helen felt abandoned and had thrown herself into her work to fill the gap. Subsequently, her friend had two children before divorcing her unfaithful husband and made contact with Helen. They began taking holidays together and regularly met for local outings but decided to remain in their separate houses. The friend lived near her grown up children and spent much of her time with them, whilst Helen still had contacts in the local hospital where she had spent most of her working life. She was aware that I too lived alone, since our helpful window cleaner had told her I was a widower and golfer after spotting my golf clubs.

Once more, our chatting had made time fly and the bar was almost empty, which showed it was time for us to go home. We walked back and as we reached Helen's house, she turned and kissed me on the cheek before walking to her door.

It was a spontaneous gesture which I assumed was for my help in giving her the guidelines for paving her garden. My body clock had not yet adjusted to the time difference with Thailand and I thought a coffee and a little reading would help me to sleep. Helen would be a good friend and neighbour and I was looking forward to working with her as we set the garden club in motion. Perhaps it would be a good time to spend a few days in South Wales and when I returned, I should contact Jean, who would know how things were moving along between Dickie and Trudy. As I slipped between the sheets, I wondered if my contacts and activities were now filling my time so well that I would have to have a priorities list.

After breakfast next morning, I rang Janice and asked if she was prepared to cook me a meal in two days' time and she insisted that I stay with her and save money instead of booking in at a local hotel. Using the satnav, I was able to find the end of terrace house in Bridgend and as soon as I had stepped inside, I was given a long kiss to welcome me to Wales. It was late afternoon and over coffee we exchanged details of our lives since our last night together in Luxor. Janice had become a grandmother and was excited about the arrival of her first grandchild. I told her about Dickie and Trudy and my plans for the garden club. She thought it would be good for Dickie to have a woman to look after him, but was not very interested in my idea for a garden club. We ate in the kitchen and the meal was really special and welcome since I had missed lunch to avoid eating at a motorway stop during the journey. Janice asked if I would like to visit the local pub and we walked down in time to take part in the evening quiz competition. As the strange man with a local widow, I had to smile as I was scrutinised and responded to questions about home and hobbies, but it was a friendly atmosphere. We walked back up the street arm in arm and passed neighbours who all knew Janice and would probably check up on me later. Janice made coffee and asked if I was happy to share a bed since her spare room had been cleared for decorating and I could not resist teasing her.

"I don't know if it would be right because I forgot to pack pyjamas and I can be restless in bed."

"You won't need pyjamas with me to keep you warm and you can be restless all night if you like after driving all that way to see me."

I woke early the next morning and as I checked my watch, Janice snuggled up to me and I relished the warmth and softness of her body against my back. It was time to say good morning and far too early to get up. Later, Janice asked if I fancied tea in bed and I told her I have never liked eating or drinking in bed, but how would she like to drive to St David's in Pembroke for a day or two. She told me she had never seen the smallest cathedral in Britain and would love to go. After breakfast, I was on my phone booking our hotel in Haverfordwest when her youngest daughter Miriam arrived unexpectedly. My impression was that the room temperature dropped suddenly and had I been a burglar I would not have been looked at with more hostility. Janice made her a cup of tea and told her about our planned visit to Pembroke and since I was totally excluded from their conversation, I left to check on my car parked outside. I stayed in the car and listened to the news until Miriam came out, saw me in the car and walked past with her face turned away. Obviously, Miriam did not approve of my presence in the family home with her mother.

Janice was very embarrassed by her daughter's rudeness and told me that she should have spoken with her beforehand about my visit. Her elder daughter knew about me and was pleased for her mother and when Miriam called to see the new baby, she told her about my visit. When Janice had asked why

Miriam had not telephoned to check that she was in, her daughter told her that she did not think she had to make an appointment to visit her own home. Obviously, Miriam had strong feelings about having her family home remain a shrine to her dead father and keep her mother a widow living alone.

Putting my arm around Janice, I told her to pack and that we would be on our way as soon as she was ready to enjoy a break in Pembrokeshire. The incident made me think about the problems Dickie had when he was engaged to the nurse. Miriam was rude, obsessed, grossly overweight and determined to deny her mother the opportunity to meet male friends. Within an hour, we were on our way and arrived at our hotel in Haverfordwest in time for lunch. Located in the centre of the town, the hotel had a small but attractive garden area and space for car parking. We spent the rest of the day exploring the town and with blue skies and sunshine it was pleasant to walk around the castles and museums. There was a good restaurant in the hotel and an attractive lounge to drink our coffee after dinner. I could tell that Janice had been depressed by her daughter's behaviour and tried to cheer her up, but she remained quiet and was obviously turning over the meeting in her mind.

Parking and breakfast were included in the hotel price and the building itself dated back to the eighteenth century. The weather was still good and the drive to St David's took only half an hour as we passed through the green countryside. I have always been interested in cathedrals and had visited many in the UK as well as the Vatican in Rome, the Sagrada Familia in Barcelona and Notre Dame in Paris. St David is the patron saint of Wales and established a monastery on the site in the sixth century. The cathedral is the smallest in Britain but very attractive and unique in lying at the base of a hill with the small village surrounding it. Since it has a cathedral, St David's village is entitled to call itself a city. Walking around the cloisters and central areas, I was fascinated by the magnificent ceiling and exquisite carvings in wood and stone. It was incredible that such skills were possessed by our medieval ancestors. I could not imagine how they had carved and then raised the large stone blocks to build the lofty tower, but I could imagine the number of craftsmen who had been killed or maimed in the process. The widows, or maimed workers, would receive no help and with no income would be permanently struggling to find food and shelter.

Janice was not as impressed by the building as I was, probably because she was still thinking about her daughter's behaviour. Taking her arm, I led her out of the cathedral and into the sunshine as we explored the ruins of the Bishop's Palace and St Nons Holy Well and chapel. We walked around the city of St David's and found a café to sit down and try the local tea. I tried to move her thoughts away from her daughter's attitude.

"So what do you think of this cathedral for your patron saint, Janice Roberts?"

"Oh I am sorry to be so miserable, but it really upset me to see my daughter being so rude to you and nasty to me as well. I am a widow now and I loved my husband, but I want to enjoy the time I have left and Miriam has her whole life before her and has no right to ruin mine."

"Am I the first man you have met, or was it because she found me in the house you shared with your husband?"

"I have met other men and you are the first to stay at my home, but I invited you and I had been hoping you would come since we met in Egypt."

"I suspect that seeing me with you surprised her and when she has time to think about it and talk it over with her older sister, she will feel embarrassed and change her attitude. After we lose our long-term partners, we have to make adjustments and so do our children. Well, Janice, I think we have been here long enough, so how about driving to Swansea and checking out all those lovely stores?"

Janice leaned across and kissed me.

"You are a very nice man and I would love to go to Swansea."

Arm in arm, we walked to the car and after spending the day in Swansea, we drove back to her house in Bridgend. Janice wanted to cook our evening meal to make up for her daughter's behaviour, but I told her it was her holiday and my treat and would she choose a local restaurant. The meal at an Italian restaurant was superb and after parking my car outside her house we sat together in her lounge and watched the evening news as we drank coffee. As soon as we were in bed, Janice wrapped herself around me and we were soon asleep. Somehow, I sensed that she needed comfort but did not want to make love.

At breakfast, Janice was very quiet and I wondered if it was because she had decided to avoid meeting me again or because she sensed that the thought was in my mind. We both enjoyed my visit and after a big hug and kiss, I drove away for my journey north. Her relationship with her daughters was very important to her and only she could decide if it was more important than finding a new man. For me, the distance between our homes would be a problem and although Janice was good company, I did not think either of us had strong feelings for the other and even if we did, we were each firmly rooted in our present locations. My holiday romance with Janice had definitely ended and I felt sure that it would not be too long before she found herself a local man to console her.

Chapter 9
Community Spirit

The long drive back to Yorkshire took almost six hours after battling through heavy traffic and road works and it was late afternoon when I stopped at a local store to buy essential groceries. I left my car on the drive, thinking that I would go out for my evening meal after skipping lunch on the journey to get home and relax. I was ravenous and fancied an Italian meal in the town restaurant. As I was putting the shopping away, I found a lasagne in the freezer which was near its sell by date and decided it would be a good time to use it. After using the microwave, I was just settling down to my hot meal and bottle of Shiraz red wine when my doorbell rang.

Helen was at the door and I invited her in and offered her wine as I apologised for eating my first meal since breakfast. She told me how unwise it was to skip meals and sat down and explained the reason for her visit as I was eating.

"I have been doing some work on the garden layout and tried to contact you yesterday and again this morning, so when I saw your car outside, I thought I would try to catch you."

I explained my long-term interest in cathedrals and told her about driving to Pembroke to look at St David's cathedral. Helen had never seen it but was aware of its history and said she hoped to visit one day. As she sipped her wine, I finished my meal and we were looking at her sketches when my doorbell rang again and this time it was Dickie at the door, who had also been trying to contact me.

"Found you at last. I missed you over the weekend and expected to find you at the pub, but Rod told me you had not been in for days. I have had to drink on my own."

"Sorry, Dickie, that you were in such poor company, but I had heard nothing from you and thought you had probably gone off with Trudy."

"Cheeky bugger. My brother died and I went to stay with my sister-in-law to sort out her affairs. The poor devil had been really ill for the last two years and we had all been expecting it. I should have called you, but when she rang with the news, I just raced off to help her. I came back on Saturday and no one knew where you were."

Then Dickie noticed Helen was sitting with a glass of wine in her hand and turned to me with raised eyebrows. I introduced them and explained that she was my neighbour and then told him about my trip to Pembroke and hoped he would not mention Janice. Handing him a glass of wine, I described the watch meeting and my ideas for the garden club. Since he was a retired surveyor, I hoped that he would get involved and we looked at the plans Helen had drawn. They were good ideas, but he said we would have to have accurate measurements for the site before settling on the layout and he would get this done. He told us that he had a programme on his computer which would allow us to design and view possible outcomes. Helen had to make a phone call and left, which allowed me to explain about Janice, but before I could ask him about Trudy, he made the inevitable comment.

"That is a very good-looking woman you were entertaining. Have you got something going for you?"

"Helen lives eight houses down from me and has a girlfriend living in Manchester and they get together whenever they can. We are close neighbours and she is interested in the garden project and nothing else."

"So how often do you have these wine drinking get-togethers with her?"

"We are neighbours and are working on a project to build a garden and that's all. Now tell me what you know about Trudy and her divorce."

Dickie told me that he had stayed in a hotel in York for a couple of days to help Trudy with her divorce application. She wanted to be sure her husband would not find out about him and they had to meet when he was away driving his lorry. Trudy was worried that if her husband knew about her boyfriend, he would use the information to reduce the divorce settlement to her. Dickie told me that until the divorce was settled, he did not have to decide about their future together, but he could not face the thought of losing Trudy. He also mentioned that he had met Jean when he was in York and she asked him to pass on her regards.

Tuesday was my usual tennis day and the rest of my week would be taken up by planning the garden club first meeting. It would not be a good time to invite Jean to come over and stay for a few days, but I decided to telephone her to let her know what was keeping me so busy. Once Dickie had left, I made the call and was relieved that Jean was in and answered. She asked about the holiday in Thailand and after giving her a brief summary, I told her about my visit to St David's cathedral in Pembroke and she was very impressed.

"You have been a busy boy. I have read about that cathedral and it must have been a very long drive because it is at the very end of Pembrokeshire. We have a magnificent cathedral here in York and it is much more accessible and I would be happy to take you on a guided tour. By the way, our tennis courts are now finished and available to play whenever you are ready."

I felt a twinge of guilt when I said that I was very involved at present and explained about the launch of the garden club and that once it was up and running, I would like to try out the new courts. I wanted to avoid hurting her feelings and told her that Sunday was garden club day, but if she was free on Wednesday the following week perhaps, we could meet.

"Wednesday evening next week, I have been invited to dinner with my retired colleagues and friends, but partners are also welcome. Would you be willing to run the gauntlet again and go along as my partner?"

"Of course. I would be delighted to chaperone you. Would that be as your tennis playing gynaecologist or your decorator?"

"Don't you dare embarrass me again. If you come it has to be as a normal, retired and well-behaved tennis playing pensioner."

"Will do ma'am. What time do you want me to be there?"

"How about playing tennis in the morning and then I can do us a light lunch and I have a few small jobs to test your handyman skills. There should be plenty of time for us to get changed for the 6.30 pm drinks before we eat. It's not black tie, the meal is in a pub and dress is informal, but no shorts or baseball caps."

We said goodnight and I had enjoyed speaking with her and was pleased to have made contact and agreed to take her to the re-union dinner. She was a lovely, undemanding lady with a strong sense of humour and I always enjoyed spending time with her. I played in a tennis match on Tuesday evening and next morning I invited Helen to my house to help in planning our first meeting at The Yorkshireman pub. I wanted to maintain momentum and avoid having our volunteers lose their initial enthusiasm. I remembered that two were rotary club members and hoped to launch stage one of the plan at the Sunday meeting. If we could have ten or more members with forks and rakes, we should be able to dig over the entire site by teatime. Everyone hates digging in the rain, but fortunately the weather forecast was good and we should have a fine day. The two rotary club members were missing, but we did have twelve people at our Friday meeting. They were all willing to come on Sunday morning with their own tools to begin the work. On Sunday, only six turned up and with Helen and myself we had eight workers to tackle the long grass and weeds. I took my fork, a rake and a pick, which from previous experience I thought might be needed. I also had large plastic bags which we filled with weeds and piled up in a corner to be taken to the council tip. Stones and rubbish were a problem. Builders often bury bottles and cans and we had to bag these separately, but we would need the stones and they were piled in another corner. By lunchtime, we had made good progress as we made our way to the pub to rest, eat and satisfy our thirsts.

When we returned to the garden afterwards, I was disappointed to find we had lost two workers, but we all kept at it until six o'clock, by which time we were all very tired and very dusty. After thanking our fellow volunteers for their hard work, I put an arm across Helen's shoulders and told her that I had a powerful multi jet shower, which I guaranteed would smooth away the aches and dust if she wanted to try it. She said that it sounded just what she needed and would collect clean clothes before coming to my house. As I opened my door, the phone rang and it was Dickie calling to tell me that Trudy's husband had somehow found out about her boyfriend and warned her that he would not be giving her money for her fancy man to spend. She was really upset and didn't know what to do. In the middle of our conversation, Helen arrived with a small bag and I put Dickie on hold while I showed her to my bathroom and explained how to stand in the middle of the power jets. After finishing the call from Dickie, I went to my kitchen and prepared a chicken salad and opened a bottle of white wine.

I finished just in time to see Helen walking into the kitchen with her wet hair wrapped in a towel as she told me about her delight with my shower.

"Thank you. That was incredible and you were right, those jets certainly do massage you all over and it really has eased my aching muscles. It was really good of you to have made this salad and opened a bottle of Chablis. Do you spoil all your neighbours like this?"

"I hardly know any other neighbours, but you have been a great help with the project and you never stopped digging away at the long grass and those terrible giant dock leaves. Most of those things seem to have roots three feet deep and even with a pick they take some pulling. Help yourself to the salad and give me about twenty minutes for me to shower and change, then if you wouldn't mind putting the coffee on, I should be back with you. Everything is set out on the worktop."

When I came back to the kitchen, I ate some salad and then found Helen in the lounge with the coffee pot and cups set out on a table. We drank our coffee and then I told her about the beautiful Welsh cathedral and my work before I retired, before listening as Helen told me about her childhood growing up in Cheshire. She also spoke about her work in the hospital and her satisfaction in bringing help to the patients. We drank all the wine and it was warm in the room and I was surprised to notice that Helen had quietly drifted off to sleep as I was telling her about the Thailand holiday. It had been a full day of hard work and we had drunk quite a lot of wine, so I was not surprised. I covered her with a blanket and headed for bed, since I was also having trouble keeping my eyes open. I had a dream that I was in bed with Janice, who wrapped her arms around me as I tried to console her after her confrontation with her daughter. When I finally woke up and checked my watch, it was eight o'clock and when I turned to speak to her, I was surprised to find myself looking into Helen's green eyes instead. She seemed as surprised as I was and very embarrassed as she tried to explain what had happened.

"I really am sorry. I woke up in a strange room and for a moment I had no idea where I was and then I thought about how much I enjoyed the day with us all working together. You have always been so helpful and considerate to me and perhaps I drank too much wine. My friend Joan has her own family and we haven't seen each other for months. I have been trying to find something to get me out of the house and then you come along and invite me to help with your garden scheme. It had been such a lovely day and you let me use your fantastic shower and prepared salad and wine for me. I couldn't leave without thanking you first and when I found you fast asleep in bed, I don't know what came over me. Perhaps it was the wine, but I felt so alone just standing there and just wanted company. I don't remember taking my clothes off and getting into your bed. When I found myself lying next to you, I realised what I was doing and was trying to leave when you suddenly turned and put your arms around me and suddenly we were kissing."

"And for me it all seemed part of a dream and it was so realistic that I didn't want it to end. You have nothing to be sorry about Helen. We are both consenting adults and it was a wonderful end to a wonderful day for us both. I do enjoy your company."

"Thank you for that Tom. I enjoy your company too, but after today we should be friends and neighbours only and if I ever need your shower again, I will definitely skip the wine first."

"You just said that *after today* we will just be friends, but I was asleep and thought I was dreaming last night and it is still today. Here we are sharing my bed together and all I can see is your wonderful green eyes."

"What happened last night was my fault and I still don't know what came over me, but now I must get dressed."

You can never get too much of a good thing, but although Helen was certainly not going to allow me to repeat my dream experience, the sight of her naked body as she jumped out of bed certainly perked up my morning. Unfortunately, my morning invitation had been rejected.

After dressing, Helen stayed for breakfast and we dropped back into our normal friendly and neighbourly roles as we worked on plans for the garden project. Neither of us made any further mention of our night together, but we both knew that whatever the circumstances, a special bond had been formed between us. We would have to find ways of raising funds to buy materials and two of our initial supporters were rotary club members. We needed their support since they might be willing to raise funds for us. Perhaps it would be possible to charge an annual fee for garden club membership, but it could be pushing too hard, too soon to ask people to do the work and pay for the privilege. If we could find a sponsor, we could display a board on the garden with the sponsor's name or two boards with the other featuring advertisements for local services. We would have to wait until Dickie produced his scale drawing before we could start creating designs, which would then be shown to members to make a choice. I expected that most would be happy to build and possibly maintain the garden but might not want to become too involved in detailed planning.

Before returning to her own house, Helen asked if my special shower had been expensive to install. I told her that the shower had come with the house and the previous owner had worked in the plumbing trade and would probably have chosen the best. As she was leaving, I mentioned that it was easily big enough for two people and she told me that since it was my shower, I could invite whoever I liked. After she left, I could not resist walking down to the garden to have another look after all our hard work on Sunday. It was bounded on two sides by the five feet high stone garden walls of estate houses, which formed a right angle alongside. The garden was highest where the two garden walls met and then it sloped down to road level, which would result in rainwater draining down to the road and washing the best soil away. It would be too much work for us to level the garden by hauling surplus earth away and our best option was to build a low retaining wall to create a gentle incline. A dry stonewall would be perfect, but would be expensive and require skill we might not have. Instead we should choose either stone or brick bonded with self-mix mortar. Satisfied with my ideas, I went off to play golf. I had often had a game with Arthur, who owned a local builders supply business and knew he normally arrived at the clubhouse around mid-morning looking for a partner. As I was lurking near the entrance, I saw him park his car and waited for him to join me. Arthur had an uncanny knack of finding his balls whenever they went into the rough, no matter how long the grass was. I wondered if he had somehow managed to fit a homing device on his balls, until one day I accidentally knocked his golf bag over. To my surprise, every ball which spilled out had the same number stamped on it. I had discovered his secret. We never played for money, but would be submitting scorecards after each round which would give him a reduced handicap and presumably bolster his pride. No way was I going to buy sets of golf balls to build a supply with identical numbers. We needed a sponsor and Arthur needed a partner for a round of golf and our needs coincided. As we swung and chipped our way around the course, I told him about our garden project and how we would have a large board showing the name of our sponsor at the entrance to the large Freshfields estate. After hitting two balls into deep rough and finding them both, Arthur won easily and we went to the bar to celebrate his victory. Over our second drink,

Arthur told me that he would be happy to sponsor our garden project. Job done and golf is only a game anyway!

It took three visits to the council tip for me to clear the black bags full of weeds and rubbish after our Sunday dig, but we were left with a large pile of stones. I hoped that when we were building the base for the wall, we could use them all as hardcore. I rang Dickie to ask how he was doing with our scale plans and was pleased to learn that they were ready. Things were moving along nicely. Stone building blocks and paving stones cost money, which we did not have, but at least we now had a sponsor. We would have to call a meeting on Sunday morning at the pub and hope that with a ten o'clock start we would have a sizeable gathering. We needed to get our list of possible designs ready for handing out at the meeting, which meant that Helen, Dickie and I would have to get to work. I spoke with Helen to update her on progress and she invited us to tea at her house on Friday to work on our designs. I had persuaded Dickie to print off a supply of scale blank garden outlines for us to work on.

Helen had prepared a delicious paella with fruit drinks, but no wine in case we fell asleep. She was looking at me as she said this and I winked at her and received a hard look in response. We finally chose five designs, all with low retaining walls at the boundary to contain the soil and take up the slope of the garden. Some had a central lawn and others had flagged paths bounded by earth areas. I was convinced that once the members had chosen a design and we had then calculated the costs, we should be able to raise the funding needed. The rotary club members could be our best source and I was hoping a lawned area would be chosen to help me to introduce further activities which would generate community spirit on the estate.

Helen was particularly charming to Dickie, who was obviously enjoying her attention and I was barely acknowledged. I wondered if it was mild punishment for enjoying our meeting in bed or a twinge of conscience on Helen's part. Whatever the reason, I knew that I had no chance of guessing or understanding her behaviour. Helen kept topping up Dickie's glass and sympathised with him as he explained the problems Trudy was having with her divorce. I was expecting him to mention Jean, but his natural caution and loyalty to me overcame the alcohol and female attention. I was proud of him.

I had already decided that I would tell Helen and Jean of my friendship with each, but at a time of my choosing. We were not married, nor in a fixed relationship with two-way commitments, but we had made love as a mutual decision, even though it had been an unexpected event. Perhaps I would eventually have to make a choice, or face an ultimatum, but for the present, I wanted to be sure that there were no secrets between us. Dickie was not fit to drive or to be driven to his home and I gave him a bed for the night. At least when he woke up in the morning, he would know that I was sleeping alone in my house and Helen in hers.

The Sunday meeting was a great success and there were thirty people who listened to our ideas and helped to select a garden design. Fortunately for me, it did include a central lawned area. Only one of the rotary club members was present, but he was very enthusiastic about our plan and said it could be a good project for his members. I made it clear that our prime objective would be to raise funds and we were looking for at least £1,000 to cover the building materials. Dickie had gone to York and when I asked Helen if she was available to work on our costs, she told me she had prepared lunch for us at her house. Afterwards, we could use the afternoon to list the items we needed, before checking prices with suppliers. I wondered if it was the right time to lose another game of golf with Arthur.

Helen was a very good cook and I complimented her on her chilli served with fruit drinks in place of wine. I mentioned that it was a good choice because wine usually made me fall asleep and Helen immediately told me that she had not noticed that effect on me, which I thought was unfair.

"I was asleep when you got into my bed with me."

"Perhaps you were, but you were certainly not asleep when you turned around and grabbed me before following your instincts."

"I am a man and reacted automatically."

"I think that enthusiastically would be a more accurate description."

"Well, it was far and away the most incredible dream I have ever enjoyed, but perhaps it would be best if we got on with our plans."

After three hours and two cups of coffee, we had worked out the number of stone blocks, capping stones, bags of cement and sundries for the building work, as well as the shrubs and lawn seed, we thought we would need. I sat back on my chair and gave a sigh of relief that it was all done. Helen told me with the planning finished, she would get out the wine, but only if I did not mention showers or beds, or even think about them. I told her that I was too tired to think of anything at all and after one glass I knew that I was ready to go home. I gave Helen a quick peck on her cheek and thanked her for her help and the meal and left to return home and enjoy a stimulating session, all alone in my shower.

Chapter 10
The Florida Keys

We three, Helen, Dickie and I checked over all the calculations for the garden materials and since Dickie still had his working contacts, he agreed to try and find the best prices. When we had priced everything, we would have a target total to put to our club members, rotary club and our sponsor Arthur, who might do us a deal on the building supplies. After Dickie left to make a start with his contacts, I told Helen about our meeting with two ladies in Cyprus and how I was happy to be an escort for Jean at her Wednesday reunion. I also told her that we had slept together. Helen looked surprised, but only for a moment before she put her hand over mine.

"Thank you for being honest Tom, but we are not in a relationship and what happened between us the other night was a result of all sorts of things coming together. I also want you to know that I have no regrets, but don't you dare use that as an invitation to get me into your fancy shower with you."

"Thank you, Helen. I will also be open with Jean and tell her about the other night. We are not in a relationship, but like you I think she would prefer to know so that she is not embarrassed if Dickie talks about our work together on the garden project. I have not and will not tell Dickie about our night together. You are a wonderful neighbour and friend and I hope we can enjoy working together and helping each other whenever necessary. I can also offer you my services as an escort, or whatever and whenever needed."

"It all depends on what services you are thinking of with that devious mind of yours, but thank you for that and I hope that you and Jean enjoy the reunion dinner."

On Wednesday morning, I drove to Haxby for tennis with Jean, who could not get her serve working and kept double faulting. She was obviously embarrassed and that only made her serves more erratic. Finally, I walked up to her and told her that from experience, I always found that when I served a fault with my first ball, I took a deep breath and moved two steps sideways. The extra time and new serving point usually helped me and luckily it also worked for Jean, who gave me a big hug when we finished playing. We went to Jean's home for lunch and she told me that my shorts were slack and she could tell that I had lost weight. I mentioned the food poisoning in Pattaya and the heavy digging on Sunday and she said the pub dinner might help. She was very interested in the garden scheme and I thought it was a good opportunity to tell her about Helen. She was quiet for a moment before responding.

"I enjoy our friendship and always look forward to our meetings, but we are both free to live separate lives and we have made no commitments to each other. From what you told me, Helen is in a relationship with another woman, which is cooling and she was probably depressed as well as a little drunk. Otherwise she would never have got into bed with a rogue like you. It was nice of you to tell me though and perhaps you are feeling just a little guilty."

"Of course, but I am here now and will do my best to be a model escort with your colleagues at the dinner tonight."

Jean looked horrified and I kissed her and said how much I was looking forward to meeting her friends, which did not seem to ease her concern. After doing one or two small repair jobs, we were sitting down when I asked about Trudy. The date for the divorce hearing had been set and she was depressed by her husband's hostile behaviour and his threats regarding her fancy man. Jean said they would both be glad when it was all over. We drove to the pub and were in good time for the 6.30 pm drink reception. I was wearing long sports trousers; my best Ralph Lauren check shirt and my hair had been cut short.

There were twelve people in total at the pub who had gathered in the private function room and all but four were ladies. One of the men had retired from teaching and the others were escorts like me. Over drinks, Jean walked me around and introduced me to all her friends and by the time we had met all of them, I had completely forgotten every name. I circulated and gave information on personal details when requested and it was obvious that Jean was very well liked. The ladies in particular seemed to be anxious to make sure that I was free and suitable. I have no idea on their opinions on me, but at least they were friendly. Having attended many drink receptions when I was working, I began with a gin and tonic and then kept topping up with tonic. I wanted to avoid letting Jean down by becoming too mischievous and I was driving her home afterwards.

During the meal, one of the ladies asked Jean when she was taking her holiday in Florida to see the Keys. Jean explained that her friend Trudy had pulled out because of domestic problems and it had to be postponed. The lady said it was a shame and looked expectantly at me, but I kept silent and left Jean to field the implied invitation. Jean told her about her friend's divorce and that they might yet go when the divorce was settled to cheer her friend up afterwards. Most of the conversations centred on time spent when they worked together and unfortunately the male escorts happened to be spaced out beyond speaking distance with each other. Unable to communicate, we sat quietly and smiled sympathetically at each other from time to time. We were simply doing our duty which would hopefully be appreciated by our partners.

As we drove back to Jean's house after protracted goodbyes and hugs, excluding partners, I was thinking about the cancelled holiday to Florida. Jean was obviously disappointed and I had always enjoyed my visits to America. If we could get away within days, a two-week holiday would not clash with garden project progress and I would like to take her. Back at her house, Jean opened a bottle of wine and told me it was a reward for my exemplary behaviour and because she knew I had drunk at least three bottles of tonic to prevent a loose tongue. I decided to ask about the cancelled holiday.

"Your friend asked about a holiday to the Florida Keys with Trudy, which was cancelled. Are you still hoping to go, Jean?"

"Yes I am. My brother spent a month in Florida and has never stopped telling me how incredible they are. I read about them and I suppose with my background in education I must have got Trudy interested as well. We had been planning a two-week holiday together, but her divorce and uncertainty about a settlement seems to have changed everything."

"This garden project I am involved in is beginning, but the real work has to wait until we sort out the funding. If you would be happy to go within the next few days, I would love to take you."

Jean threw her arms around me and hugged and kissed me and I could see that she had tears in her eyes. I had never seen her so emotional.

"Wow. Don't stop, Jean, I love it. So, I can take that as a yes, can I?"

Jean was speechless with emotion but nodded her head and told me that she was going to the bathroom and that it must be time for bed. I put the stopper on the wine bottle and went to the bedroom, undressed and got into bed. My head had hardly touched the pillow before Jean returned and was astride me and enthusiastically showing her appreciation for my holiday offer. I knew that I would enjoy the Florida Keys with Jean, but not as much as the wonderful show of passion for taking her there. We fell asleep only when we were too exhausted to continue and remained locked in each other's arms. It had been a very enjoyable day and I was struck by the similarity between Jean and Helen. Both were confident and capable women but demanding nothing and becoming emotional when they were shown appreciation or kindness.

Once we had finished breakfast, we went on line to book our flights from Leeds Bradford Airport to Miami and I arranged accommodation for our first three days at the Miami Marriot Hotel. This would give us a base and we could then arrange car rental and explore the state. Florida thrives on visiting tourists and those in the know use the 'walk-in' system. When calling at a hotel in mid-afternoon and asking for a walk-in booking, it is possible to book any free rooms at a discount. If no discount is offered, there are lots of other hotels in the area happy to oblige instead of having unused rooms. I had been to Miami on business but had never found time to explore the many attractions and surrounding areas and often thought about visiting the Keys. We were booked on a Friday flight, which only gave me one day to brief my helpers to look after the garden club development for the coming two weeks. Dickie and Helen were very surprised that after just coming back from one holiday, I was now off on another. I emphasised that it was a late flight booking at a good rate and the Keys had been on my must-see list for some time. I also told them that Jean and Trudy had planned to go until the divorce changed everything and I wanted to help Jean. Helen's only comment was that I was always the good Samaritan.

Miami Airport had become more Spanish than ever. All notices were in English and Spanish and as we were surrounded by fellow passengers, I could hear them all speaking Spanish. The Americans had taken over the area from Spain, but there was a gradual return to the previous language and customs. Our hotel was alongside the beach and there was an outside swimming pool surrounded by palm trees in the garden. After a twelve-hour flight, we were hot and sticky and I persuaded Jean to go for a swim in the warm water. There was a strong but warm breeze blowing in from the sea and it was really pleasant to soak up the relaxing atmosphere. We changed for dinner and heard that there was a hurricane moving in from the Caribbean, but it was not expected to travel in our direction. Hurricanes are unpredictable and Jean was worried that on our first day we could be involved in a tropical storm. We were given a room on the twenty-first floor and I reassured her that we should certainly be safe from flooding. During the night, the noise of the storm was so great that it woke us both as wind howled around the building and buffeted our windows. I asked Jean to get on top of me again to stop me blowing away, but she told me to wear earplugs and turned over. Scorned and unable to go back to sleep, as soon as it got light, I dressed and went to see the storm.

The receptionist at the front desk told me that the hurricane was passing closer than anticipated but would still avoid Miami and if I was going outside, I should be very careful and keep hold of the safety rails. The front doors would not open because of the wind strength, but I was shown a rear entrance which was more sheltered. It was still a struggle to open the door and I had to crouch and grip the handrail to move outside. The wind was bending the palm trees almost double, so that their fronds were brushing the ground. With my first sight of the sea, I was amazed to watch the enormous grey waves rushing towards the beach and shocked to watch surfers struggling out into the wild waves before coming racing back on their surfboards. I was watching the waves, which was just like seeing boiling water in a pan, when suddenly a small metal pole flew past and was followed by other items hurled through the air by the force of the wind. Should they strike anyone, it could well be fatal and I thought it best to get back to the safety of the hotel. When I returned to our room, Jean told me that she had been worried because I had been mad enough to go outside. At breakfast, we sat near a window and looked out on the broken trees and shrubbery after the passing of the storm.

The nearest key, or island was Key Largo which was one hundred and sixty miles south from Miami. Looking at a map, we chose instead to drive north to St Petersburg first and then return and make our way down the keys to Key West at the very tip. By lunchtime, the weather had returned to normal and we visited the large Cuban area in Miami. The locals were fun loving and in colourful dress, as well as being really happy to have escaped from the rigid communist regime of Fidel Castro, which forced most of them to exist in poverty. As we were standing near a promenade, a large group of people suddenly began to dance, beat drums and sing and then invited us to join in. Cuban cigars were banned in America, but many of the local men and women seemed to be smoking the giant cigars or some very good copies. We joined a tour which took us to Miami Beach and included a boat trip along the many waterways where we passed the multi-million-dollar mansions with most having their very expensive boats moored alongside.

Next morning, we set off west along the Everglades Parkway, which is also known as Alligator Alley. Through the car windows as we drove along, we were able to see rivers and canals alongside, with alligators basking in the sun, or drifting in the water. Jean wanted to stop and get out of the car to have a closer look until I told her that on dry land these amphibians can run as fast as a horse over the first twenty yards. We did stop, but stayed inside the car with the windows wound down. The 75 motorway goes north and crosses over Tampa Bay via the Sunshine Skyway Bridge, which is over four miles long and 430 feet high to allow ocean liners to sail beneath. Driving up to its highest point, the car bonnet is pointed up at the sky and it is almost like flying. I had to keep my eyes on traffic on the three-lane roadway and Jean opened her window to look down at the ships passing below. The wind then blew all loose papers and other items around inside the car and she had to close it. We booked in at the Hilton Hotel, St Petersburg Beach and only had to walk out onto the beach alongside to watch dolphins leaping and diving in the sea. It was an ideal location.

Next morning, we began exploring the area by driving north to Madeira Beach and parked alongside John's Pass, which has a long wooden boardwalk for fishing alongside a wide selection of shops, bars and restaurants. We were watching the fishing boats come back after their early morning start and suddenly saw dozens of large pelicans fly down and perch on the handrail. One actually waddled up and nudged me out of its way and looking down at its enormous beak, I kept my distance. As the fishermen gutted their catch and threw the scraps into the air, the pelicans flew up and caught them in their beaks. The birds obviously knew when to expect the boats and flew in to await their arrival before jockeying with each other for the best positions. Looking out into the bay, we could see more dolphins diving in and out of the water as we stood on the boardwalk, with well-fed pelicans now missing. We ate dinner at Sculley's Fish Restaurant on the boardwalk. The meal was delicious and our table window overlooked the shimmering blue waters of Tampa Bay. It was a wonderful way to spend our evening.

Jean was enjoying every minute and told me that she felt like a young girl again, but I discreetly avoided making the inevitable male response. It was wonderful to see her so happy and although the magic of Florida was the main reason, it was good to have helped to make it possible. We had become very comfortable in each other's company and I noticed that Jean was smiling and laughing more than ever. We all deserve a special treat now and then to bolster our spirits and bring the fun back into our lives and the holiday was doing this. At the end of three days visiting the beaches, piers and resorts along the Gulf Coast, it was time to move south and make our way to the Keys. It was a long journey and halfway we stopped off at Naples for two nights. The Naples Hilton was just across the road from a very large nature reserve, or as the Americans call them, nature preserve. It looked worth a visit, but we wanted to explore the town first. Naples had a splendid white sand beach and a small pier as well as the usual shops and lots of restaurants. Jean was worried that with the fabulous meals we were enjoying she would get too big for her clothes without lots of exercise and so we went swimming every day. I offered to carry out regular body checks, but I was told I was already making quite enough.

We spent our second day in the preserve, which had a zoo and a large lake. Taking a boat trip on the lake, we passed some small islands where we could see monkeys and what we were told were lemurs. I was surprised that they did not escape into the water and wondered if they were unable to swim. The guide told us that they could swim but knew that if they did enter the water, there were hungry alligators waiting for them. We left the boat just in time to stand at the side of the lake as a bell rang to summon alligators for feeding. A female ranger was standing on a tall wooden platform projecting out over the lake to ring the bell. We could see dozens of alligators swimming under the platform and waiting for their food to arrive. When the ranger tossed meat down to them, some leaped six feet out of the water to catch it ahead of their rivals, while others fought each other to get the food. Watching the large reptiles leaping over each other and churning up the water, Jean was worried that if the platform collapsed, the ranger would fall down amongst these monsters and it would be impossible to save her. I assured her that there must be regular safety checks to avoid this ever happening.

Naples was a great place to spend holiday time, but we had to push on to the Keys and left early the following morning. We booked in at Key Largo and again our hotel was at the side of a beach and after dinner we sat on a jetty and looked down at the fish swimming below us in the clear water. Our first venture was a boat trip up a river leading into the Everglades and our guide was another female ranger wearing a Stetson hat and high leather boots. She told us that in this fresh water there were only alligators, but where the river emptied into the sea there were larger and more powerful crocodiles. I asked her what happened when these two amphibians met and she explained.

"The crocodiles are much bigger and more powerful and they wait for the alligators to arrive and eat any which come their way."

I told Jean that there were likely to be very few alligators in the sea as a result but wondered why the crocodiles did not swim up the fresh water river to eat even more alligators. Mangrove trees with their long, twisted roots showing above the water line are salt tolerant and grow alongside both fresh and saltwater areas. They lined the riverside and we watched as cormorants, ibis, cranes and other birds perched in their branches. There are also brown bears on dry land areas and venomous snakes both in the water, on the land and even in the trees. Recently Burmese pythons, which are mainly escaped or discarded pets, have found their way into the area and have no known predators and can grow to twenty feet in length. The ranger explained that they do not normally attack humans, but Jean was not happy and said she would not leave the boat until we returned to the dock. The ranger heard this and immediately reassured her that she had not lost a passenger yet. Jean was not convinced and hung on to me and I was happy to tell her she was safe with me and enjoy the moment, as you do.

We left Key Largo to drive along the single highway leading to Key West at the very end of the Keys, which took us over two hours. The Spanish had built a fort at the edge of the sea and the town seemed to be a mix of Spanish and French buildings, which were tightly packed and included no public parking areas which I could find. We parked near the fort and walked back to the town, but found either that there were no vacancies, or the price for accommodation was ridiculously high. We decided to look for accommodation further back along the Keys and booked in at a motel alongside the highway in Islamorada, which had a row of bungalow wooden chalets for guests. This small key was flanked on either side by the sea and had a large swimming pool and sandy beach at the rear. There was no restaurant, but we could see a typical wooden shack and fish restaurant only a short walk away where we ordered clam chowder soup, followed by locally caught lobster. At the food store, we bought snacks and cold drinks to take back to our chalet. It had a small veranda with chairs and a table and we finished the evening sitting in the sun and reading. Motels often include small kitchen areas with a microwave and refrigerator, which are useful for families or long-term guests, who buy groceries locally and eat in.

The highway links each island key with the next as it uses bridges to cross over the sea between and when driving this gives the impression of driving along a pier. In the morning we ate a continental breakfast available in the motel main building, used the waffle-making machine for the first time and naturally swamped them with syrup. We could choose either syrup, or jelly (jam) to flavour them and followed the American tradition by adding syrup. As usual it was a hot sunny day and we walked to the pool for our swim and were surprised to find that there were no other swimmers. As we approached the steps, we noticed a very large iguana crouching alongside and watching us with its hooded, bulging eyes. We circled around to approach the pool from the other side and the iguana turned so that it could continue to glare at us. At least I thought it was glaring, but who knows with these creatures. I reassured Jean by telling her that at least it was not actually in the pool and perhaps we had interrupted its morning warm up in the sun. Jean was adamant that it would probably dive in if we invaded its water area, which was probably why there were no other swimmers. We walked past to swim in the sea and left the three-feet-long reptile glaring after us. Jean had read that their bites were always poisonous and said that the sea looked really inviting and would be better than swimming in the pool. I stopped myself in time and did not mention sharks.

The sea was warm and the sand was soft and suddenly I felt the hot sun on my back and insisted on smoothing sun cream on us both. Jean was adamant that she would not remove her top to get tanned all over, or nearly. She always wore a one-piece swimsuit and after watching her, I thought it was not quite the tight fit I had admired in Cyprus. She certainly had no reason to worry about growing out of her usual dress size in spite of all the delicious meals we were enjoying. After our swim, we were lying on our towels and I was surprised to hear my phone ring. I always keep it with me in case of car breakdowns, or attacks by iguanas. It was a good connection and I recognised my eldest daughter's voice. Her first question was to ask where I was and I described the beach we were lying on, which she complained was a dream location compared with her cluttered kitchen and wet weather in Yorkshire. I was told that I was now a grandfather and I was delighted to have my first grandson. She and her husband had wanted children for some time and with the help of IVF treatment they had finally succeeded. I told her that we still had a week to go, but I was looking forward to meeting our new family member. Later at the local store, we looked for champagne to celebrate but could find only bourbon, beer, cola or root beer. We settled for another lobster dinner instead.

From Islamorada we drove back along the Keys to Miami Beach to spend our final days within easy reach of the airport for our flight home. We chose a hotel alongside the vast sandy beach, which was near a large shopping mall we visited to buy bargain priced American goods. The Florida tax was only 6%, which is added after you make your purchase, instead of having it included in the sale price as in the UK with our value added tax. After swimming, shopping and eating we went for our last visit to the mall. I bought a couple of Ralph Lauren check shirts and Jean bought clothes for herself and Trudy, which meant that we would also have to buy an extra suitcase to take them home with us. She picked up a smart pair of ladies stretch jeans and asked what size I thought Helen was. Looking at Jean, I told her they were of equal height, but Helen was perhaps a size bigger around the bust and hips. Jean told me they were very good quality and would cost twice as much in England. She thought they would be an ideal gift for all the help Helen had given me. It was a lovely thought and one that I should have considered myself. I added the jeans to our purchases.

Our holiday had ended and we had both finally made it to the Florida Keys and many other incredible locations in the Sunshine State of America. We had both thoroughly enjoyed ourselves, but it suddenly dawned on me that sharing the experience with Jean had made it so much more special. I knew that I had strong feelings for her but could not make up my mind whether they were developing into love.

Chapter 11
The Fairfields Garden Club

Next morning, we were on our flight home with our extra suitcase and our Florida tans and after collecting my very dusty and bird spotted car from the car park, we drove back to Haxby. Jean cooked a light meal and unpacked and although we hoped to stay awake to reduce the five-hour time lapse with Florida, we gave in and went to bed instead. We were up early the next morning and over breakfast I asked Jean when she would like to come and stay with me. She would then be able to meet my new grandson and look at our part prepared garden site. Her reply took me completely by surprise.

"Well, as they say, there is no time like the present, so if you will have me, why don't I go back with you today? I can't wait to meet the new baby."

We drove to my home after dropping in at the local supermarket to buy groceries to last us for a week. As Jean was putting everything away for me, probably in the wrong places, I began opening the dozen or so letters delivered during the holiday and was surprised to find one from Janice. Her daughter Miriam had realised that her behaviour during my visit had been rude and unforgiveable and she wanted to apologise. Since I had no plans to visit Bridgend, I would not be meeting her or mother, Janice. We walked down to the garden to look at the expanse of cleared brown earth and piled up stones after our hard work. I explained how we were going to lay out the walls and lawn area when we had the money and hopefully bury all or most of the stones. It was now a reasonable time to drop in on my daughter Karen and I drove Jean to her home in my car. I introduced the two and they seemed to take an immediate liking to each other. Karen said that I had been keeping Jean a secret for far too long. After a career in teaching children, when she was allowed to lift my grandson, I could see the joy in Jean's eyes and wondered how disappointing it must have been to have no children of her own. Karen asked about our holiday and was busy feeding the baby as we told her about our time in Florida. Younger daughter Abby was at work, but wanted to meet Jean during her visit and would ring me or call in. At least my daughters would now be relieved that I was not falling into the hands of designing women.

I suggested having dinner at The Yorkshireman pub so that Jean could meet my friends, but Jean insisted on cooking because it made a change from cooking only for herself. Telling her that we would have to visit the pub to meet the locals, we skipped wine with the meal and walked down after clearing everything away. I was now so used to washing my few dishes after each meal that Jean was startled when I took her plate away to be washed as soon as she put her fork down. Jean met Rod and the other regulars, but Dickie and Helen were absent. According to our neighbourhood watch controller, Dickie had gone back to visit his widowed sister-in-law to sort out some legal problems and he thought Helen was in Manchester. After finishing our drinks, we walked back to watch a TV programme Jean was following. After visiting my bathroom, she was fascinated by my high-tech shower and before going to bed and as a special treat guaranteed to make her glow all over, I offered to initiate her. First, she had to take all her clothes off and stand in the middle so that I could soap her all over, before turning on the jets. I made good progress until I received a complaint.

"Oi. You have already soaped that part four times."

"You know how I always try to do a thorough job."

"Yes, and I can tell how much you are enjoying your work, now turn around because it's my turn."

After showering together and feeling rejuvenated, we went to bed and made good progress in cancelling our jet lag from the overnight flight back from Florida. The airline provides a blanket, eyeshade and slippers as well as turning down the cabin lights, but I still find it almost impossible to sleep when folded up in the airline seat. Next day, we played tennis together and drove to Hawes to visit the Dales and tour a cheese factory. We were sitting in the Yorkshireman when Helen walked in and came to join us at our table. I introduced them to each other and went to get a drink for Helen as they began chatting. The two rotary club members were at the bar and we were soon involved with their plans to raise money for the garden project. Whenever I was able to glance over at my table, the two heads were close together and I hoped I was not the subject of their intense conversation. When I was finally able to break free without cooling the enthusiasm of my key cash raisers, I sat down with Helen's drink. They both laughed and Helen told me that Jean now needed a top up, but she would get it in case I got lost again. When we all had drinks,

Helen asked about Florida and told us that her only visit had been to Orlando and how much she had enjoyed strolling around the Epcot Centre. In the company of two determined ladies, I judged it would be unwise to ask why she had missed out on meeting Mickey Mouse. Helen said she was tired after the drive back from Manchester and we decided to follow her. Jean seemed unusually quiet and after we had coffee, she made her way to bed.

Over breakfast next morning, Jean asked if I would mind driving her back to Haxby, because she had things she needed to sort out after coming to stay with me so soon after returning from Florida. I was disappointed that she was cutting short her stay but thought that she was probably anxious to help her friend Trudy. When we reached her bungalow, I parked on her drive and carried her case into the house and since she seemed to be very much in a hurry, I turned down her offer of coffee. She told me she was going to visit Trudy and gave me a very long kiss on her doorstep before I left to drive off. When I got back home, I found younger daughter Abby standing beside her car on my drive. After giving me a hug, she told me she had come to meet Jean after visiting Karen and the new baby. I explained that Jean had to return home unexpectedly to help a friend and that next time she was visiting we must all go out for a meal together. We had coffee and I told her about the Florida holiday before she left.

I rang Dickie and Helen and asked them to meet me at The Yorkshireman. Helen arrived first and she too seemed quieter than usual and I began to wonder if it was just me, or were my two lady friends both having miserable moods. Fortunately, I remembered to bring the jeans we bought in Florida and gave them to her with my thanks for all her help. She held them up and told me they must have cost a fortune, before asking how I knew her size. I described how I simply compared her with Jean. As she thanked me and gave me a quick peck on the cheek, I was surprised to see tears in her eyes. Once Dickie had joined us, I began telling them about recent progress on our Fairfields garden.

"I met our two rotary members at the pub and they told me they had planned a gala day at the local park to raise money for us and for other charities. Although the garden would replace an eyesore in the area, they preferred to raise money for charities, or to help the community. I told them that once the garden club was up and running the new garden would be just the first of a number of local community services we had in mind. I hoped to persuade our members to give their time on a regular basis to tidy gardens and cut lawns for those residents too old, or infirm to do so themselves. It might also be possible to have capable members carry out small repairs, such as broken windows, or fences for needy residents. The rotary men became very enthusiastic and said this was an ideal scheme and would get their full support. Unfortunately, I have not yet put this idea to our club members and we need an early meeting to get their approval."

Dickie shook his head at me and could not resist commenting.

"You are flying by the seat of your pants again my friend. What if our newly recruited members are not interested in extending the scheme to help other residents?"

"We will just have to prepare our plans and work together to convince them that it is a wonderful opportunity to make Fairfields estate the most neighbour friendly in the area. We could call our meeting at 10 am on Sunday morning, which we know is a popular time and if I can persuade our sponsor to provide us with free building materials, we can start building the walls and paths the following Sunday. Once we have the money, we can order the bench, shrubs and grass seed and so on to be planted later. Rod is busy running his pub and as neighbourhood watch coordinator, but I would be willing to run the garden club. I think we should circulate all the Fairfields estate residents with information on the meeting and since we need to be available for contact throughout the week, would you be willing to help me on this Helen?"

After a rather long pause, Helen replied that she would be willing to help out. We began by e-mailing residents and covered the remainder by putting leaflets through their letterboxes to get as many as possible to attend the Sunday meeting. I was at the golf course in good time to offer Arthur a round of golf and told him about the full role the garden club would play and how during contacts with residents we would distribute leaflets showing his company name as sponsor. Speaking with him in the bar after our game, I showed him the list of materials we would need to build the garden. After carefully looking over the list, he gave it back to me and said he would deliver them all free of charge as our sponsor. I could have hugged him, but shook his hand instead and could barely control my excitement. As soon as I was home, I rang Helen and Dickie with the news and Helen suggested we should meet at the pub and seemed to be in a brighter mood. I wondered what sort of reception she had faced with her girlfriend in Manchester to make her so depressed. I was sitting at a table with my Timothy Taylors beer in my hand when Helen arrived and I was pleased to see that she was wearing the American jeans I had given her. I told her they looked really good on her and bought her a drink. We sat quietly looking at each other before she broke the silence.

"I heard nothing from my friend in Manchester and when I went to see her, the moment she opened her door and I saw the annoyed expression on her face, I knew that it was all over between us. She invited me in and gave me tea as she told me of her intention to marry again. The news did not come as a surprise, because she failed to reply to any of my e-mails and it had been many months since we last met at her home. She had been married before and it was not a success and ended in divorce. I had boyfriends myself but did not see any of them as lifetime partners. We had been friends for years and after her divorce we came together and now it is finished. You should be pleased because now I will have nothing but free time to help you with your garden ideas."

"Helen, please. You know that I would never be pleased about anything which made you unhappy. I count you as one of my very special friends."

"I know and I'm sorry I said that. It's just that she has been part of my life for so long and now it has been taken away. I can do nothing about it except find new things to do and new people to meet to fill the gap and get on with my life."

"I understand because I have had to do the same thing and you have made the right decision. We are going to be pretty busy over the next few months and I will need your support."

Dickie arrived and when he heard that our building supplies would be provided free of charge, he congratulated me on pulling my irons out of the fire and said we could now go ahead. My business experience taught me the importance of advertising and after receiving Arthur's generous offer, I rang our local councillor, who agreed to attend our meeting. My next contact was with a local reporter I had met playing tennis and after giving him details of our plans, he also said he would attend. We should get free publicity, but needed a good turnout at the meeting to make it newsworthy. Rod allowed me to put a large notice up in the pub and with our leaflets distributed throughout the estate we had done all we could to draw people in. I also invited Arthur, who should be acknowledged for his generous support.

It was all worth our efforts and there were more than sixty people at the meeting and I told Rod he should have his best Sunday morning bar sales ever. Hearing my ideas about looking after the older people on the estate, there were many volunteers ready to join in and our local councillor said this was good for the community and he would do whatever he could to help us. I could see the reporter writing in his notebook and hoped he was giving us a good write up. I had also mentioned the gala day which should bring in more visitors and help to boost our funds. The garden building work could now begin next Saturday with a small team digging the footings and using the stones and cement as hardcore for the wall base. We could then build the retaining wall on Sunday. Later that evening, we three were sitting in the bar and congratulating ourselves for a successful outcome. We were joined by Rod, who brought us two free bottles of wine to join us in a toast before being called back to his duties. Dickie soon followed him after saying he was worn out by the suspense. Anxious to avoid drinking too much and being accused by Helen of having ulterior motives, I invited her to my house for coffee. To my surprise, she nodded her head and said it was a good idea.

Over our coffee, Helen asked if I had spoken with Jean recently and I was ashamed to tell her that I had been so involved with the garden meeting that I had not found time to call her. Hearing my admission, she began to tell me about her conversation with Jean at the pub.

"We had never met before, but we took an immediate liking to each other and spoke openly. She has strong feelings for you, which she does not think are reciprocated. She enjoys spending time with you and is happy to continue with your loose relationship for as long as you want to be with her. She told me how you had brought laughter and excitement into her life which had been missing for a very long time. I think she is a very lovely person and I would not want you to hurt her."

Helen's words shocked me and I assured her that I would never knowingly hurt Jean, or any other woman I met. I also told her that I felt guilty about not keeping in touch and would telephone her first thing in the morning. Next day, I had to take my car for service, but telephoned at 10 am from the garage. Trudy answered my call and told me that Jean had gone away and she was looking after her house.

"Where has she gone, Trudy? I thought she was helping you with your divorce proceedings."

"She came back from staying with you and said she had to go down to her brother for a week or two and asked me to look after her house."

"Is her brother ill?"

"I think he must be because Jean was in such a hurry to drive down to Kent to be with him. She just had time to give me the keys and explain about the burglar alarm and then rushed off."

“Do you have her brother’s address or a contact number I can call?”

“No. She told me she would ring me when she had settled in and wanted no calls to avoid having her brother bothered.”

“OK. Thank you, Trudy, and would you mind letting me know when Jean does call you and let me have a contact number.”

After switching off my phone, I wondered how serious her brother’s illness must be to send Jean rushing off in such a hurry. At least I now knew why she had suddenly cut short her visit with me. Everything seemed to be happening at once. First the gala in the park, which was a big success on a very sunny Sunday. There were lots of stalls and competitions and the local brass band to entertain everyone. With the large number of people who attended, the takings were well above expectations. There was a generous sum for the garden club and for other charities supported by rotary. We had a large team of willing workers on the Saturday and Sunday to build the wall and level and spread the grass seed for the lawn. Shrubs were also planted and the bench was bolted into concrete to form a sitting area at the highest level. Perhaps one day I would be glad to sit there and enjoy the sun as I watched people passing.

Stage one was complete and it was now time to organise the help service to needy residents. Helen worked hard and always seemed to be alongside me. I guessed that she was determined to keep busy until the hurt from losing her girlfriend had passed. We got on really well, but Helen kept her distance as far as personal relations were concerned. I told her about my conversation with Trudy and the problems with Jean’s brother in Kent. She nodded her head but said nothing and I didn't know whether this was because she was jealous of my meetings with Jean or because she wanted to keep her distance because she liked Jean. Either way, we seemed to be getting along quite well and I was looking forward to meeting Jean again when she was ready. We had another meeting to report on progress and arrange a schedule of members to keep the garden and lawn in good condition. We were also ready to begin receiving requests or nominations from elderly, or infirm residents whose gardens needed attention. The last item on the agenda was a name change to Fairfields Garden Club, which would avoid confusion with any other garden club.

Everything seemed to be going well and I was thinking of easing off or taking some sort of away break when Trudy called. Her voice was so choked with emotion that at first, I could hardly understand what she was telling me. She had just been contacted by Jean's brother, who told her that Jean's cancer had spread and she was not expected to survive much longer. He asked her to contact me and tell me that Jean wanted me to remember her as she was in Florida and not as she was now after the failed chemotherapy treatment. She also insisted that I must not try to visit her because that would leave me with the wrong memory of her instead of the one from Florida. I put my phone down and felt the tears trickle down my face as I realised just how much Jean meant to me. For the second time in my life, I was about to lose a woman I loved and as I was busy with my schemes, Jean was fighting her losing battle with cancer. I rang Dickie with the awful news and he was just as surprised that Trudy seemed to have been completely unaware of the illness or its severity. We believed that Jean had kept the news from Trudy because of the strain it would put on her in having to keep it secret.

It was late afternoon and I needed company instead of sitting alone at home and blaming myself for all the things I should have done or said. I had been so determined to protect my independence that I was blind to my own feelings for Jean. If she had known my real feelings, I might have helped her and stayed with her during the treatment. Dickie joined me in The Yorkshireman and we were sitting in silence and gazing into our glasses when Helen suddenly sat down beside us with a drink in her hand.

"You two look as if you are drinking sour grapes and when I came in and looked over, I thought it wise to come prepared with my drink. I expected you to be drinking champagne after all the success with the Freshfields Garden Club."

I gave her the news about Jean and she immediately apologised for her comments. I told her that she could not have known and that she had nothing to be sorry about. After sitting quietly for a moment, she surprised us with her comments.

"When I met Jean here with you and while you were lost at the bar, she told me that she had been diagnosed with cancer and advised to have chemotherapy to halt the spread. She knew I had been in nursing and asked me about the effects.

"I told her about the hair loss, vomiting and weight loss and urged her to tell you. She wanted to keep it from you and made me promise to say nothing. She had fallen in love with you in Cyprus and could not believe it could happen to her after so long and at her age. After thinking that she would never get to the Florida Keys, you took her and those two weeks were the best she had ever known. She wanted to leave you with that memory instead of seeing her fade away. She knew she had little chance of recovery and wanted to stay with her brother to have her treatment. Her life with her husband was miserable and after her divorce, she accepted living on her own until you brought fun, excitement and love back into her life. If she had not found out about her cancer, she hoped that you would gradually come to love her as she loved you."

I could not contain my emotions and had to apologise and leave them to go back to my house and grieve for the woman who deserved so much and had to accept so little. If only Jean's pride had not prevented her from telling me her true feelings, or could it be that she saw my determination to remain uncommitted as a barrier. Perhaps I had been wrong to tell her about the night I spent with Helen and encourage her to say we were not in a sole relationship. In spite of drinking more wine than I should have, I failed to get to sleep that night.

Helen called in to see me as I was clearing up after breakfast. Probably noticing the bags under my eyes, she asked me if I had been able to sleep last night and was not surprised when I shook my head. She told me that Jean had a premonition that she would not survive the cancer and knowing that we were close friends, she asked Helen to keep an eye on me. After the conversation with Jean, she was upset, which was why she left us at The Yorkshireman so suddenly. A few days later, she found that she had lost her long-term friend and had been trying to escape from a black cloud ever since. Jean told her she did want me to see her as the illness progressed, but I could not let her die without saying goodbye. Helen was adamant that if I ignored Jean's request, she would be devastated that I would be left carrying a memory of her diseased body, instead of the memory of her she wanted me to have when she was in Florida. I knew she was right, but I had to battle with my feelings to accept her advice. Two weeks later, we were at the funeral in York with Trudy and Dickie. Jean had left her house, money and possessions to Trudy so that she now had her independence, whatever the outcome of the divorce. I wondered how her newfound independence would affect her relationship with Dickie.

Chapter 12
Route 66

The press coverage given to Fairfields Garden Club and community services brought a surprising number of offers of assistance and free materials from private and business followers in the area. We were asked to speak to other communities who were interested in copying our style of garden scheme. I persuaded Helen to carry out as many of these as possible to keep her busy after the break with her girlfriend and because of all her hard work. Trudy had originally agreed with Jean to look after the bungalow but was now remaining to make it her new home. Also, she was now in no hurry to move to a more permanent arrangement with Dickie. As ever, when you cannot have what you want, you want it more and Dickie had now become very keen to make Trudy his partner. After accepting that Trudy wanted to move ahead more slowly, he told me that since my schemes were all running well it would cheer me up to go on an exciting holiday which he had in mind. He also pointed out that while I was sunning myself and living on lobsters and thick steaks with Jean in Florida, he was left on his own in Yorkshire. I could not believe that he would ever be on his own for long, but was willing to listen to his proposal.

Dickie had seen an advertisement for a journey across seven American states along Route 66, from Chicago in Illinois to Los Angeles in California, which was roughly 2,500 miles. He was obsessed with wanting to drive a Ford Mustang car and had checked on the cost of hiring one for the journey. Unfortunately, because the car would be taken across seven states, he would then have to pay the cost of returning it to Chicago, which was very expensive. He then found a travel company which ran guided coach tours along the route, taking fourteen days unless extra time was added at the beginning or the end of the tour. He showed me the brochure and it named quite a few locations I was interested in visiting. Putting his arm across my shoulders, he told me that we would be so busy checking out all the sights on this trip that it would help to take my mind off what happened to Jean.

"I know you are right, Dickie. I must be miserable company at the moment, but I now have the Fairfields Garden Club responsibility and I can't just go off and abandon it. It has only just started."

"Look, Tom, I know you think you are indispensable, but it is only for two weeks and it will do us both good. Why not ask Helen and Rod if they will fill in for you?"

I agreed to go, but only if Helen and Rod would look after things in my absence. We spoke with Rod first and he wanted me to get away and was willing to help, but with his limited free time he asked if we could also persuade Helen to keep herself available so that they could work together. When I spoke with Helen, she was sympathetic about giving me a break and change of routine and told me that I had done a great job in launching the FGC and she would be happy to look after it for the two weeks while I was away. I gave her my records and told Rod, who told me to go away and enjoy myself. Helen had become a big part of my daily life and without all her help and support it would have been very much more difficult to set up the FGC. After the breakup with her friend in Manchester, I could sense that she had distanced herself from me, but she was always willing to help with work on the garden project. Now I had the feeling that she was beginning to be more relaxed in my company.

I told Dickie to get us enrolled on the Route 66 tour and booked us on an American Airlines flight from Manchester to O'Hare airport in Chicago. I had previously flown there on business before transferring to the smaller Midway Airport for flights to Minneapolis. It was a ten-hour flight and on arrival we took a cab to our hotel on Michigan Avenue. Dickie had never been to Chicago before and after checking-in, he was keen to see as much as possible of the Windy City. Our hotel was in the centre of the city alongside most of the big stores and with a large selection of bars and restaurants. At my suggestion, we added two days at one end of our tour and three at the other so that we could see more of Chicago and Los Angeles. We walked down Michigan Avenue to find a typical American bar and Dickie kept away from the bright neon clad cocktail lounges. At last we stood outside a plain stone-faced building with the brass-lettered name of 'Griffin's Bar' and he said it was the one. We walked inside and stood at the bar as Dickie ordered two Miller Lites, the only America beer he knew. Looking up, I was startled to see a full-size Harley Davidson motorbike suspended from the ceiling above us. Then I looked around the bar and saw that it was filled with large bearded men with leather jackets festooned with brass studs and wearing high leather boots. I also saw that they were all staring at the two strangers who had invaded their select group and were now standing at their bar.

Turning to the barman, I tried to think of something to say which would break the silence. Pointing at the motorbike hanging above our heads, I smiled and spoke to him:

"Nice bike you have there. We don't see many of those in Britain."

I watched carefully as a smile slowly broke out across his bearded face. I might have missed it, but my eyesight is still quite good, probably due to playing tennis regularly.

"Oh. You two guys are Brits."

"Yes. We are here in Chicago to start our tour across Route 66. We were hoping to ride across on Harley Davidsons, but after crossing seven states, we would have to pay to get them shipped back to Chicago and it was a lot of money."

The bearded bikers all came down to the bar and I could see the Hells Angels signs on the back of their jackets as they welcomed their biker allies from across the pond. They would not let us pay for any drinks as fellow visiting bikers and we spoke about British, German, Japanese and Italian motorbikes. I had only ever owned two British motorbikes when I was young and unable to afford a car, but I had read about all the more powerful bikes which I dreamed of buying. Fortunately, their details still remained in my memory. After an hour or so, I knew that if we did not leave while we could still walk, we might have to be delivered back to our hotel by Hells Angels. We said goodbye and gave our thanks to our American allies and fellow bikers and headed back down Michigan Avenue. It seemed a very long walk, but we finally reached our hotel. Dickie told me that as he noticed the silent stares around the bar, he was sure that we would also end up hanging from the ceiling alongside the Harley Davidson. He then told me how very impressed he was by my theoretical knowledge of world motorbikes, which fortunately for us had roused the interest of our hosts.

At breakfast, I translated the American menu for him and he ordered eggs benedict and pancakes with maple syrup. Every time our waitress passed, she topped up his giant coffee mug and I told him to put a napkin over the top, or he would spend the morning looking for the 'John' or toilet. We walked through Grants Park and saw the enormous fountain, which is similar to the one at Versailles in Paris. At intervals, a giant column of water erupts from the centre of the fountain to shoot forty feet into the air. Smaller fountains are set around the sides to squirt water into the centre and there is also water spouting out of the mouths of stone lions. After waiting to watch two water eruptions, we walked alongside Lake Michigan, which stretched as far as we could see and noticed very large ships crossing the distant horizon. Our destination was Navy Pier, which during the Second World War had been a US Naval base and stretched far out into the enormous lake. It was two miles long and we found theatres, museums, children's play areas, bars and restaurants on our long walk to the pier end. I looked around at anglers sitting patiently with their rods reaching far out into the lake, with pelicans perched nearby and hoping for a share of the catch. Checking the many empty tubs beside the fishermen and intended for their catch, the fish were obviously doing a superb job of dodging the baited hooks, or were unhappy with the menu. We took a boat trip on Lake Michigan and were able to look back at the incredible skyscraper skyline of Chicago before heading for the entrance to the green coloured Chicago River, which passed under the city as well as flowing alongside its giant buildings. The tour ended at a pier under a bridge on Michigan Avenue and was only minutes away from our hotel.

Our next attraction was the Chicago aquarium, which has two viewing levels. At the lower level, we watched as eight dolphins built up speed and surged up to and through the water surface to vanish from sight. At the higher level, we saw the same dolphins shoot out of the water in perfect formation as they rose ten feet in the air before diving back down again. After a coffee break in the restaurant, I told Dickie I had always wanted to go to the top of the Sears/Willis building. It was 1,450 feet high and had 110 floors, but I even had difficulty persuading him to mount an escalator and he insisted that I go alone. He was happy to wait at ground level and have coffee, or a beer. I took the long journey up in the lifts to the viewing platform, before walking around and looking out through the giant glass panels at the clouds drifting past alongside. Peering between the clouds, I looked down at the city below and wished the day had been clearer, when it might have been possible to see for fifty miles. Finding Dickie at the coffee bar, he did not want to hear about my time amongst the clouds.

We had often seen the Chicago overhead railway, or Loop in American films and as we walked beneath it the trains clattered along above our heads. I suddenly noticed two Chicago policemen in their black tunics, leather belts and holstered revolvers, who seemed to be walking straight towards us. I stood to one side to let them pass, but they stopped and stood facing us. One policeman spoke to me:

"Where are you guys from?"

The weather was warm and sunny and we were both wearing shorts and light jackets and I guessed we looked like typical tourists. I told him that we were in Chicago from Britain to travel along Route 66. The other policeman spoke to us and said he was born in the US and had still not made that journey. They told us we were in the drug district, where two German tourists were mugged three days ago and one was still in hospital. It was not a good place to go walking, particularly when it was just starting to get dark. They suggested we take a cab back to our hotel and when I thanked them, one raised his hand to a passing cab, which pulled alongside us and we were glad to jump in. As we drove off, I gave them a thumbs up and hoped it meant nothing rude in American usage. Back at our hotel, I was not impressed by the bland restaurant menu and instead we walked to a Chinese restaurant across the avenue and enjoyed their fantastic Cantonese cuisine. Our stay in Chicago was almost over and tomorrow we would board our coach for the long journey along Route 66.

Our coach was a large American model with two wheels up front and four at the back and included a toilet and small kitchenette built in to the rear. There were forty passengers instead of the sixty capacity, which allowed some to take up a double seat to stretch out, or spread their belongings alongside on the vacant area. Most were British, but there were also Canadians and North and South Americans. The majority were couples and amongst the singles, as usual on tours, most were ladies. Our guide, Luis, travelled with us and was an American Hispanic who lived in Las Vegas, which was on our route. Our first stop was at Springfield to tour the

Abraham Lincoln Mansion and we watched as guests were introduced to a bearded actor dressed as the former president. We were amused to watch as visitors lined up to shake his hand, as if he were a reincarnation. We noticed that wiser and unimpressed fellow Brits kept their distance and silence.

I had heard the song *Meet me in St Louis* and we finally made it, but unfortunately, we didn't meet anyone. Standing where the Missouri and Mississippi rivers join together, the city is a major port on the inland waterways system and an industrial centre. The Gateway Arch is made of aluminium and rises 630 feet above the ground in downtown St Louis. I had read that it was possible to ride inside the arch to the summit and as Dickie found a bar near the river, I climbed on a sort of chain with seats and was taken up inside the giant tube. At the top, there were tiny windows to allow viewing of the city on one side and the Mississippi River below on the other. Having experienced a bird's eye view of St Louis, I climbed back on the chain to return to ground level. Grand Central Station had been mainly converted to an indoor shopping mall, with cafes, bars and pleasant sitting areas. Only a small part was still used for the cross-country rail link. Noticing that the traffic was being stopped whilst people were gathering at the roadside, we waited to see what was happening. We watched as a parade of Shriners passed down the road with men wearing red fezzes on top of their heads and driving very small single seater cars. The toy cars were followed by full size open top Cadillacs, with ladies in the back wearing wide brimmed red hats. Speaking with a local, we learned that the Shriners were associated with our own Masons and raised money for charities and in particular The Shriners Children's Hospitals. The ladies were from the Red

Hat Charity. It was the first entirely motorised parade we had ever seen, but in America the car is king.

On our way west, we stopped at the Meremac Caverns in the Ozark Mountains and while I took the tour, Dickie took to the bar. The network of caves extends for four and a half miles, with incredible displays of stalagmites and stalactites, pools and a giant cavern as big as a cathedral which is used for concerts. The guide told us that Jesse James and brother Frank once hid in the caves with their gang and horses and as a sheriff's posse waited for them at the entrance, the brothers escaped by riding out through a previously unknown exit at the back. We continued on our way to Oklahoma City, which was very large and very modern. During the journey, Dickie sat near a friendly lady from Norwich. She had been drinking with him in the bar instead of also taking the Meremac tour. Nadia and her friend Christine worked in the council offices in Norwich and were making their first visit to America. Nadia was divorced and Christine was unmarried and had just lost her mother the previous year, after taking care of her for many years. We reached our hotel in the late afternoon and checking on local services, Dickie saw that there was a gun club not far from our hotel. We decided to pay it a visit.

I had never visited a gun club open to non-members before and was impressed by the modern building and racks of guns available for customers to select. We each booked one hundred round sessions with handguns on the range and Dickie chose a Glock and I favoured a Sig Saur. We stood in our separate enclosed channels and took aim over 25 yards at a bull's eye target. As I fired off my last round, I noticed a body silhouette target appear in the next channel, with a heart drawn on the chest. After a steady stream of fifty shots, the heart outline had completely vanished, which was very good shooting with a handgun. Waiting until the man stepped out of the channel, I went to congratulate him. To my surprise, I saw that he was a state trooper in a well-pressed fawn uniform, with high leather boots and holstered gun. We shook hands and he told us he was Sergeant Pete Rawlins and he invited Dickie and me to join him for coffee.

Pete had been in the US Army stationed in Germany and had relatives in the UK. I asked if the Sig Saur he was using was his gun, or one hired from the club. He told us his police gun was crap and three weeks previously, he had shot a man involved in a robbery and hit him, but the man kept running and got away. He had just purchased the Sig and was very pleased with it. He was also not happy with his Harley Davidson motorbike, which was police issue and spent more time in the garage than on the road. For his pleasure riding, he owned a Honda Gull Wing, which I knew was a very luxurious and very expensive motorbike. Pete could not understand how the UK police were able to maintain the law without carrying guns. He was also amazed that UK homeowners were not allowed to defend themselves with guns against intruders breaking in to their properties. We assured him that we preferred fewer guns in our country, which had prevented the mass shootings experienced by Americans. As we were leaving the gun club, he gave us his card and told us that if we had any problems while we were in Oklahoma State, we should produce it. Oklahoma State is a major oil producer and as our coach drove along the highway, we could see nodding donkey derricks, which pump oil out of the ground twenty-four hours of every day.

A special dinner was laid on for our coach party at our hotel and following this our guide gave us a choice of either visiting a local movie, attending a hog roast, or visiting a casino. Dickie had not seen a film in years and was not keen on the hog roast. Instead and together with four ladies, he persuaded me to go with them to the casino. During my business career, I had been to a number of casinos and they wanted my guidance on losing their money. I agreed to take them, but only if they promised they would leave their credit cards in the hotel and only take the money they were prepared to lose. We travelled in a stretch limousine and entered the magnificent building built with money gathered from unlucky gamblers. The group scattered amongst the tables offering a range of games and I chose French roulette, which I had played before. Betting on even versus odd numbers, I stayed roughly within my fifty-dollar limit, but when I changed to selecting groups of numbers instead, I was soon down to my last ten dollars.

I watched a Chinese gambler put money on my French roulette table and then cross over to another roulette table nearby, where he also laid his bets. As I watched the croupiers scoop up his money on both tables, I wondered how long he would be able to sustain such losses. I decided to put my last ten dollars on my birthday date and closed my eyes as the wheel began to spin. I listened as the small ball clip clopped around the numbers on the spinning wheel until it finally stopped in a numbered slot. I opened my eyes and expected to find I had lost my money, but incredibly it had settled in my birthday number. I had just won $320 and after giving the croupier $10, I was still well in profit and walked away quickly before being tempted to stay and lose it all. I went over to where Dickie, Nadia and Christine were just leaving the Blackjack table. After seeing their gloomy faces, I had no need to ask if they were winning. The last hand took the rest of their money and we looked around for the other two ladies who had come with us. We found them in the bar trying to forget their losses and they told us how their evening had gone. Initially they had won, but then their luck changed and with a string of losses they were left with no money. Ignoring my advice, they had both used their credit cards to purchase a large quantity of chips and had a number of good wins. Then they began to lose and hoped that they would again hit a winning streak, but it never happened. Both lost large sums, which they were too embarrassed to reveal, but they seemed to have plenty of money and always chose expensive wines with their meals. They lived in the Croydon area south of the Thames and jointly owned two hairdressing salons. On our way back to the hotel, Gloria and Dorothy assured me that in future they would follow my advice, but I was not convinced.

Driving across the Painted Desert, I saw my first tumbleweeds. I had heard of them and now I watched as these dried balls of weed the size of footballs rolled along as they were pushed by the wind. We were in the state of Texas and stopped near the metal bodies of ten Cadillac cars, which were half buried in the ground so that their rear halves pointed up at the sky. Our coach stopped and our guide gave us a selection of paint spray cans and invited us to use them to put our own designs and signatures on the exposed car bodies. Dickie concentrated on geometric designs and I chose palm trees and fishes. I found it very difficult to draw clear images with a spray can and realised why graffiti always looks so hideous, although the artist Banksi seems to have produced superb pictures on walls and buildings. After being given special cleaner to get the paint from our hands, we returned to our coach for our next stop, a visit to a cattle ranch. On our way down the long driveway to the ranch house, we passed cattle grazing on the sparse grass and as I looked around, there were no signs of buildings or people as far as I could see. Luis told us that the ranch we were visiting extended over three thousand acres. When we arrived at the large ranch house flanked by barns and other buildings, two cowboys rode up on horses. Watching them sitting astride the magnificent animals and wearing their wide brimmed Stetson hats and leather chaps, they seemed to have ridden straight out of a John Wayne western film.

We were introduced to the owner of the ranch named Eleanor, who was a buxom blond lady in her sixties wearing jeans and high leather riding boots. We all gathered in an enormous barn and sat around on bales of straw as she told us about running the ranch after her husband died in an auto crash. Texas was short on rainfall and there were sometimes dry periods when there was not enough water for her stock. When asked how she coped, she explained that she reduced their numbers in dry spells and increased them when there was enough water. On her 3,000-plus acres at present, she was running a herd of five hundred cattle. There were also white-tailed deer on her land, which competed with her stock for the limited grass available. Fortunately, they were Eleanor's chosen prey when hunting and made good cooking steaks. Texas had more white-tailed deer than any other state and the numbers exceeded three million. She told us her high boots were useful when accidently treading on rattlesnakes, both for protection and for stomping on their heads. She kept anti venom serum in case of bites and had never had a fatality on the ranch. About half of the snakebites were dry, or without venom, but she always used the antidote in case they were the other half. There were alligators in Texas, but none on her ranch, probably because of the shortage of water.

We were challenged to a horseshoe pitching competition and allowed three pitches. I watched one of the ranch hands demonstrating how to pitch the horseshoe onto a foot-high iron spike target. He held the shoe so that the open end faced towards the target. When my turn came, I did the same and the shoe hit the iron spike and dropped down with one edge just touching it, scoring one point. My second dropped short and my third landed perfectly around the spike, scoring three points. My score of four was the highest yet and Eleanor told me I must have a good eye. I closed one and pointed at the other and she burst out laughing and gave me a hearty slap on the shoulder.

Next, we watched as the cowboys whirled their rope lariats above their heads and then tossed the whirling hoops to drop around the neck of a wooden bull's head with horns. Only one of our group managed to lasso the woodenhead, but quite a few hit it with their lariats. Fun over, we were invited to sit on benches with attached tables to enjoy ranch cooking from the kitchen, which was disappointing because I expected to see the cooking done in a traditional wheeled wooden chuck wagon as in western films. My T-bone steak overlapped the sides of my plate, but was the best I had ever tasted and the apple pie with cinnamon was delicious. At the end of an enjoyable visit, we said our goodbyes to Eleanor and I got a big hug as I was crushed against her ample bosom.

"Bye, honey. Now you take care of that good eye and come again anytime you are in Texas."

Dickie was standing alongside Gloria and told her that wherever we went, I seemed to get along well with the ladies. Gloria told him that she would be quite happy to have me get along well with her too.

It was a relief to arrive in Albuquerque and stretch our legs, before checking in to our multi-storey hotel and then freshening up with a shower after hours sitting in the coach. Even though our coach was equipped with air conditioning, as we travelled across the vast arid countryside of Texas, I could feel sweat trickling down my chest. In the evening, we were scheduled to travel on the Sandia Park Aerial Tramway, which crossed over the Rio Grande Valley to ascend to the peaks of the Sandia Mountains. As usual, Dickie was unhappy about travelling in a cable car across a valley, but with the help of the four ladies who had been with us in the casino, he was persuaded.

The large cable car carried up to fifty passengers for a fifteen-minute ride to make the two-and-a-half-mile crossing. There were two cars and when one went up, it passed the other going down. As we moved out into space, I looked down at the forest far below and noticed the wreckage of a TWA passenger plane crash which was still visible. The peak was 10,378 feet above sea level and its slopes were used by skiers in winter. There was a Mexican Grill and an expensive restaurant to serve visitors who arrived to study the incredible views over the surrounding area. We had been advised to take warm clothing, but even so were still chilled by the big drop in temperature on the outdoor viewing areas. Anxious to move away from the biting cold, we were glad to hurry indoors and enjoy Mexican spicy food and tequilas. After drinking steadily, Gloria sat beside me and began moving her body against mine at every opportunity. Then she startled me by telling me that we should see more of each other during the tour. Dickie was listening and gave me a big wink. As usual, he had also tried too many tequilas and was hardly aware of the return cable car journey, which was a relief for us all. We had now formed a small group including Nadia and Christine from Norwich and Gloria and Dorothy from Croydon. We all got on very well, but I wondered if two single men could remain uninvolved for the remainder of the tour, particularly since Gloria had already shown she would like closer relations.

Driving through the Painted Desert, we crossed into Arizona and after driving for mile after mile across the flat, treeless and arid landscape, the coach stopped to allow us to visit the Petrified Forest. The forest was formed when the trees were first buried under volcanic ash and then enclosed under silt and water for millions of years to become coloured stone logs and stumps. The exposed faces have a glossy glass like finish and because tourists have helped themselves to samples, some fifteen tons have been lost. Signs now warn of fines and penalties for removing pieces of the stone wood. On our way to Flagstaff, our next stop was at Meteor Crater, which is a mile wide and 570 feet deep. It was formed some 50,000 years ago when a 300-ton meteorite struck the ground and displaced 175 million tons of earth which surround the impact crater. We climbed down a very long run of wooden steps to reach the bottom and as we looked around the sides of the giant crater, we imagined the force of the impact when the enormous meteor hurtled into the earth from outer space.

Climbing back to the surface, I looked down at the small human figures at the bottom of the crater and marvelled again at the raw power of nature. Gloria had appeared at my side as I stood at the bottom and was still with me when I returned to the top. She was not out of breath and I said that she must be fit. On our way back to the coach, she told me that she did a lot of riding because she was a golf widow.

"My husband would play golf all day if he could have food and drink delivered to him on the course. He plays with Dorothy's husband, another golf addict and when we are not working together, we go riding or spend our time at the gym. Our men were off on another golf holiday in Florida, so we decided to try the Route 66 tour. You look pretty fit yourself, what is your secret?"

"I play tennis every week and golf when I have time, because for the last couple of months I have been busy working on a community garden."

Gloria looked puzzled and wanted to know more and I explained how we had established the Fairfields Garden Club. She thought it was a wonderful idea to bring people together and told me that apart from Dorothy, she did not know any of her neighbours and would like to get involved in anything that was not connected with golf courses. She took my arm and said she and Dorothy had hoped to meet some interesting men during the holiday, but were not impressed by the other male passengers. She was obviously following up on her suggestion that we should see more of each other and with forty people sharing a coach and couples sharing rooms, I wondered what she had in mind. Perhaps I should warn Dickie against more room swapping and hope he did not become too interested in Dorothy. These two ladies had quietly moved in on us and edged out Nadia and Christine, who had first introduced themselves, but could not match the confidence or drive of the ladies from Croydon.

Our next stop was Flagstaff where we would spend the night before a very early start the next morning to be in position to watch the sun rise over Grand Canyon. It was late afternoon when we arrived at our hotel and we were scheduled to dine in and watch a cabaret. We had to have a quick shower and change of clothes before arriving at the crowded restaurant, with only the tables at the back against the wall still available. We had just ordered our drinks when Gloria and Dorothy joined us in their striking, but rather short cocktail dresses and sat on either side of us. I offered to move so that the two ladies could sit next to each other, but Gloria insisted that she would prefer to sit next to me. Hearing this, Dickie elbowed me in the ribs. The meal was very good and we shared bottles of wine and chatted away about our previous holidays. Dickie told them about my performance with the belly dancer on the Nile and I described his Thai beach massage and they envied our exciting holiday experiences. The compere came on stage and introduced the first performer. The lights gradually dimmed to allow a spotlight to shine on a tall blond in a sheer black dress. She began to do a Marilyn Monroe take off as she sang *Diamonds Are a Girl's Best Friend*, which reminded me of the lady boy act in Phuket. As we were listening, Gloria put her hand on top of mine and intertwined her fingers between mine. I was surprised but said nothing. She then took my hand and placed it on the inside of her leg and as I was wondering how to react, she moved my hand up between her legs and held it there. Her flimsy underwear provided little cover and before I could force myself to pull my hand away, or not, the singer finished her performance to loud applause and I whispered to Gloria:

"The lights are coming on. Better let go of my hand and pull your skirt back down."

Gloria released my hand and kissed me on my cheek before straightening her skirt. The lights came on again and as the audience applauded, the singer left the stage and a country and Western group came on to entertain us. I glanced across at Dickie and saw that he and Dorothy were holding hands and watching the new singers. Gloria took my hand again.

"Did you like that?"

"Yes, but it was a bit of a surprise."

"And do you like surprises?"

"Yes. Sometimes."

The entertainment ended and Gloria suggested a nightcap in the bar, but I reminded her that breakfast was booked for 5 am so that we could check out, board our coach and be at the southern rim of the Grand Canyon as the sun rose. She nodded her head and opened her arms and asked if she was going to get a goodnight kiss. As I kissed her, she pushed her tongue into my mouth and pressed herself against me. We went to our rooms and as I was undressing, I told Dickie what had happened when the lights went down.

"You, jammy bugger." Dorothy pressed her leg against me and took my hand, but I thought she was just being friendly and didn't think it was an invitation. Dorothy told me Gloria lives in a big house and her husband is retired but made a lot of money working in banking. He is quite a bit older than her and is more interested in golf than her. My guess is that she is lonely and hoping to find a lover during the tour and you are the one. I wonder if Dorothy has also been neglected and is looking for a lover. I gave him my own thoughts.

"If they are both looking for lovers, Las Vegas is the place to be and we arrive there tomorrow and our hotel is in the middle of the attractions."

Very early the next morning, we stood on the southern rim of the Grand Canyon and watched as the blood red sun just tipped above the horizon and began to light up the sky. Gradually its rays moved across the ground, but the deep canyon was still in black shadow. As the sun rose higher, its rays began to slowly reach down the sides into the abyss below and the majesty of the Grand Canyon began to unveil as we watched. The sheer sides descend a mile to the Colorado River below and the canyon is up to eighteen miles wide and is 277 miles long. The Colorado River began marking out its course five million years ago and continues to flow through the giant channel it carved out of the earth. Fortunately, because of our early arrival, we were able to stand at the edge of the southern rim and look down at the full extent of the canyon. After being transfixed by the sheer magnificence of the views above and below us, we went to the restaurant for coffee, doughnuts and the essential call at the men's room. Gloria and Dorothy remained at our sides throughout the morning until they both veered off to visit the lady's room.

We were now offered a choice of returning to our coach to drive across the Hoover dam, which held back the Colorado River to form the enormous Lake Mead, or flying over the Grand Canyon to reach our hotel in Las Vegas. There were helicopter flights along the canyon, or flights above the canyon in twin-engine planes holding eight passengers. Dickie refused to fly by helicopter, but I persuaded him to try the twin-engine plane after reminding him that he had already flown across the Atlantic Ocean. As soon as we made our choice, Gloria and Dorothy also booked flights on our aircraft. Nadia and Christine thought the cost was too high and decided to remain with our coach for the journey to Las Vegas. We boarded the plane with five other passengers who were all Americans. It took off and rose high above the canyon before banking and turning so that it could fly along its length. The pilot wanted to give the passengers a good view and tilted the plane so that we were looking down the left wing to the bottom of the canyon below. Dickie gripped the seat and turned his head away. The pilot then circled and tilted the other wing to give passengers on the other side of the plane the same breath-taking sight of the canyon. We were not issued with parachutes and I was relieved that Dickie would not be able to leap out of the plane but also wondered what would happen if the engines failed. Fortunately, Dickie was too busy fighting off airsickness to have similar concerns.

When we landed at Las Vegas airport in Nevada, there was a minibus waiting to take us to the Stratosphere Hotel, which has 2,427 rooms as well as the tallest tower west of the Mississippi at 1,149 feet. As we were all booking in, Gloria asked the receptionist if her room could be next to ours as we were friends. The receptionist was happy to oblige and Dickie's eyebrows rose noticeably. We were booked to watch a performance by the look alike Ratpack of Dean Martin, Frank Sinatra and Sammy Davis in the afternoon, but the evening was open to our own choice and we wanted to visit Caesar's Palace on The Strip. We had lunch in the revolving hotel restaurant at the top of the tower, with incredible views of Las Vegas and the surrounding countryside. There were two rides available at the tower top and one, Insanity, whirled riders out into space alongside. Dickie could not even watch and I was not tempted to try it. There was also a large pool at the hotel and I said it would be nice to cool off with a swim. Gloria said she had her swimsuit and would like to join me.

We sat through the Ratpack performance, supposedly Dean Martin, Sammy Davis and Frank Sinatra and Dickie told me they were the poorest singers he had ever heard. Luis overheard his criticism and said they were always very popular with his passengers. Dickie had once played guitar in a band and explained to Luis that he should know the difference between good and awful singers. Luis shook his head and muttered something which we could not hear, but I guessed it was probably something uncomplimentary about picky English tourists, who had also been unimpressed by an Abraham Lincoln reincarnation. After watching the Ratpack, Gloria wanted to swim and we left the theatre to return to our hotel. Dickie and Dorothy preferred to take a cab to Fremont Street at the lower end of Las Vegas. The couple wanted to visit The Golden Nugget Casino to look at the giant gold nugget on display, which was mined in Australia and is eighteen inches long. Gloria took my arm as we walked back to our hotel and suggested that instead of going for a swim, we could always go to her room, which had stunning views. She was an attractive and vivacious woman and very few men could have refused such an invitation and I was not one of them.

We lay in each other's arms with just a single sheet over our bodies to protect us from the powerful American air conditioning blast. Gloria told me how she had studied hard and been recruited into a large London broker's office and eventually became a junior executive. At the time, it was very much a man's world and she gradually accepted that she could not expect to reach a top position. She had boyfriends, but having concentrated on her career, she felt too old to marry and start a family. One of the partners was widowed and although he was twenty years older, they began going to concerts and dinners together until eventually she became his wife. He was a generous husband and she had her own car and horse, but after the marriage, she found her husband considered lovemaking and outward shows of affection to be something for teenagers. Eventually they moved into separate bedrooms and lived separate lives. When her husband wanted to go to America to play golf in Florida, she persuaded him to allow her to join Dorothy to take the Route 66 tour.

She had never been unfaithful and would never embarrass her husband by having an affair near home, but she wanted some fun and excitement in her life and hoped to meet someone on the tour for a holiday romance. She waited for me to take the initiative, but when I kept my distance and the tour was nearly over, she had to force my hand so to speak. As I listened, I saw Gloria in a totally different perspective and suddenly felt genuine affection and sympathy for her. Checking my watch, I was disappointed to discover it was time to get dressed. "Right, Gloria, first one in the shower gets to do the soaping."

Gloria shrieked and headed for the bathroom, but I made sure I was first. We spent a warm and wet time soaping and massaging each other before getting dressed and making our way to the ground floor bar to meet the others. As we were drying each other after our shower, she told me that she had never shared a shower before and it had been a wonderful afternoon. I wondered if she still believed that security and a wealthy older husband was a better choice than a younger and more affectionate, lower-income husband. Most women in her loveless situation would already have taken lovers to make up for the lack of affection at home.

We were just finishing our coffees when our friends returned and told us all about Fremont Street. They wanted to go back at night to view the incredible roof top display and we agreed to go with them the following night, since Caesars Palace and the other spectacular casinos were our first priority. We had the smallest sized American meal on the hotel menu before beginning our walk along the casino-lined road. A man suddenly jumped out in front of Gloria and whipped open his raincoat to flash her with his bare privates. Gloria laughed and pointing at his manhood told him her young nephew was better blessed. Shocked by her response, the man fled and we carried on laughing and walking. The big pyramid shaped Luxor was our first call and we were impressed as we looked up at the open tiers of floor levels around us, with the guest rooms all accessed by galleries. Moving on, we watched the scores of fountains swaying and dipping in tune with music at the outdoor pool beside the Bellagio and the gondolas gliding around the miniature canal of The Venetian. We also stopped to admire the displays at Paris with its scaled down Eiffel Tower. We finally reached Caesar's Palace and the ladies did not at first notice that the cloud designs on the ceilings changed, just like real passing clouds. We sat down near a small fountain and I asked them to watch for any movements. Suddenly Gloria shrieked as the stone statue beside her came to life and then others began to move and make slow, jerky changes in their positions. After a few minutes, the statues gradually returned to their original shapes and once again became immobile. Gloria clapped her hands with joy and was in a very happy mood.

So far none of us had tried any of the dozens of amusement machines on display in all the casinos. The ladies had kept away from them because they were probably still embarrassed about the money lost in the casino in Oklahoma City. I thought it would be a shame to stay in Las Vegas and not risk a little of our money to try our luck.

"Well, girls, why not risk say twenty dollars each by trying some of these machines?"

We spent the next ten minutes feeding US quarters into the slots and we had our wins, but more losses and Gloria was the only one to end up with a ten-dollar profit. Dorothy, believing we had spent the afternoon in the pool because Gloria's hair had been damp from our shower, teased her friend.

"Lucky with money and unlucky with love, Gloria."

"Come on, Dorothy. Ten dollars is a very poor substitute for love and I think mine is worth far more than that."

As she was speaking to her friend, Gloria was pressing her leg against mine and I guessed that she was anxious to keep our afternoon liaison secret, in case Dorothy mentioned it to her husband. Somehow, we would have to find more time to go swimming together and possibly wear our swimsuits for a minute or two in the shower. We walked through three more casinos before returning down The Strip to our hotel and were surprised how far we had travelled during our wandering. Entertainment was provided in every casino we visited, without charge and for those gamblers glued to their stools in front of an amusement machine, free drinks were also delivered. Casinos wanted to attract and retain visitors to keep their gambling incomes as high as possible. Once back at our hotel, after a very busy day, we were all ready to go straight to our rooms to sleep. I thought it unwise to tell Dickie about my swimming break because somehow it would feel like being disloyal to Gloria.

Following another typical American breakfast, with Dickie eating his way through two large waffles, the tour party was taken to a small theatre to watch and listen to Elvis Presley, presumably another reincarnation. We watched as a tall olive-skinned young man with a mass of well-greased black hair plucked at a brightly coloured guitar and gyrated his body, whilst singing Elvis songs. When his act ended, Dickie and I agreed that although the man sounded a little like Elvis, his weak voice failed to come as close as his appearance. Neither of us had ever been enthusiastic Elvis Presley fans, but enjoyed his recordings. We were then taken into a small museum with a range of Elvis's glittering jackets and trousers on display. There were also brightly ornamented guitars and an enormous chrome encrusted Cadillac driven by Elvis. Next, we were invited to meet the singer, who was sitting near the entrance waiting to sign autographs. Without exception, every British tourist walked straight past and left a surprised reincarnate with pen poised until colonials and others stopped to accept his signature.

Our afternoon and last evening in Las Vegas were free for us to choose, but Luis had arranged a bus tour to the Hoover Dam, which would include a visit to the interior and its enormous turbines, as well as a chance to walk along the top of the giant dam with its spectacular views of Lake Mead. Incredibly, Gloria told us that she could never get really comfortable on bus journeys and she would prefer to relax at the hotel. I was not surprised to hear this and said that I had really enjoyed my swim and would like to stay and spend the time in the pool again. Dickie as an ex-surveyor was very keen to visit the dam and Dorothy had been disappointed to miss it during our flight from Grand Canyon and said she would join him. The coach left after lunch and I waved my friends off with my swimsuit and towel in my hand for authenticity. As soon as the coach drove off, I hurried up to Gloria, who was waiting in her room and wearing only the terry towel dressing gown provided for guests by the hotel. As soon as I closed her door, she threw off the gown and welcomed me.

Since it might be our last chance to be alone together, we took full advantage. As soon as we had dressed and were about to go down to the ground floor for coffee, Gloria gripped my arm and spoke to me:

"This has been my best ever holiday and the scenery has been fantastic, but I have to tell you that the pool in this hotel is rubbish and the showers and soap dispensers are incredible. I will never embarrass my husband, but I have a life to lead as well. If you happened to visit London, or I happened to visit Yorkshire, do you think we could meet up if we had each other's mobile numbers?"

Unwisely as it happened, we exchanged mobile telephone numbers and went down eighteen floors to the coffee lounge. There was still an hour to go before the tour to the dam returned and I suggested we try the pool. It was big and although there were some visitors relaxing alongside, we were the only swimmers in the water. Gloria was a good swimmer and we completed quite a few lengths together before I raced ahead and was holding on to the pool rail when Gloria came up behind me and looped one leg around mine. I was about to tell her it was time to get dressed when she slipped one hand down inside my swim trunks and demanded a kiss. I was in no position to refuse and was struggling to regain possession of my property, but with one hand on the pool rail, I could not force away Gloria's tenacious grip. She made sure it was a long kiss and pushed her tongue between my teeth before releasing me and suggesting we return to her bedroom. I managed to pull myself free and point at my watch.

"Gloria, they will be back in twenty minutes and we don't have the time."

Gloria laughed and called me a spoilsport but accepted that it was time to climb out of the water and get dressed. I fancied a beer for my dry throat and Gloria thought she might try a champagne to celebrate our afternoon. We were just finishing our drinks as the two dam visitors returned. It was time to get changed for our bus journey to Fremont Street. Forty minutes later, we were dining at an Italian restaurant on the street and planning to look at the enormous Australian gold nugget that Dickie had told us about. Having enjoyed a very good meal, we stood on the street and looked up at the glass roof, which covered its entire length. Not long after it got dark, the roof became illuminated to form a giant screen and then psychedelic images flashed along its length. The climax came when a full-sized image of a jet fighter roared down and over our heads. I was getting a sore neck from twisting to watch the displays above me and noticed that some spectators were lying on the floor, which was dry and surprisingly clean, possibly to allow this. We returned to our hotel by bus and after drinks in the bar, went to our beds for our last night in Las Vegas.

Next morning, we were off to California and the end of Route 66 at Santa Monica Beach. Dickie and I were booked in for three nights at a hotel in Los Angeles, but after their meal at Santa Monica, the tour party was taken to the airport for flights home. Gloria and Dorothy, both kissed us goodbye, but when she kissed me, Gloria pushed her tongue into my mouth, gave me a special smile and urged me to ring her. I like London and a flight from Leeds Bradford Airport to London Gatwick airport takes less than an hour, which is shorter than it sometimes takes me to get to Manchester by car.

Our hotel was close to the centre of LA and there was a station for the metro rail system within easy walking distance. We took the metro to Olvera Street in the heart of the Mexican Quarter and walked around the large market square to the sound of Mexican music coming from the many cantinas on the square. There were stalls selling enormous Mexican sombreros and brightly coloured blankets, as well as dolls and skull and skeleton trinkets. We stopped to listen to a Mexican band strolling around the square wearing very large sombreros, flared trousers and blankets hung over their shoulders. We were happy to put money in the container waved at us by a pretty young woman collecting for charity who was working with them. Looking around the square with its very old gnarled tree, a two-layer stone fountain and Hispanic atmosphere we could well have been in Mexico itself. We chose a restaurant just off the main square, which had a varied, but reasonably priced menu on display outside. When we were seated in one of the booths, we boldly ordered burritos, but to save burning our tongues we asked the waiter not to make them too spicy. After being assured that it was only mild, we still had to cool our throats with Lupulosa Mexican beer, but we really liked the flavour. It had been another full day and I had trouble keeping my eyes open as the metro rail took us back to our hotel.

Next day, we took a bus ride to the Getty Centre, which is housed in an ultra-modern building on a hilltop just outside LA. It was a forty-minute journey and we had to rely on fellow passengers to tell us where to get off. The centre contains sketches and drawings, as well as sculptures and paintings and has an attractive terrace with clear views to Los Angeles. We took another bus ride to the La Brea Tar Pits, which are filled with oil which has seeped out of surrounding rocks. Some 40,000 years ago, the pits trapped a range of prehistoric animals, including mammoths and sabre-toothed tigers, which fell into the twenty-three feet deep oily water. At the time, only one of the pits had been excavated and the relics were on display in the on-site museum. We spent an afternoon at the large Farmers Market, which had an incredible selection of fruit and vegetables, as well as jewellery, clothes, watches and electronics. Having lunch at one of the many cafes, we met up with fellow travellers from Ireland, who were returning home on the evening flight. For me, the best attraction in the city was Skyspace, which was a 1,000 feet high viewing platform on top of the US Bank Tower, giving full views of LA and the surrounding areas. Once again, Dickie kept his feet firmly planted on the ground below as I rode the lift to the summit.

On our final day, we took the metro rail to visit the Queen Mary ocean liner, now used as a hotel and museum and paid a visit to Graumans Chinese Theatre to try our shoes in the footprints of famous celebrities in the pavement outside. We skipped visiting Disneyland and Universal and spent the time on Santa Monica pier, where I tried and failed to get Dickie to take a ride on the Ferris wheel. Early the following morning, we were on our way back to Manchester Airport and the train home to Yorkshire. I sat next to a lady from Manchester who had been visiting her daughter in LA. During the long flight, it helped to pass the time as we exchanged information about our backgrounds and hobbies. Diane was widowed and was very much involved in local affairs. She asked a lot of questions about the Fairfields Garden Club, before inviting me to come and visit her local community group to speak to the members. We exchanged telephone numbers and I promised to get in touch. Dickie was listening beside me and whispered that I was like a flypaper, collecting ladies phone numbers wherever I went. He was right about the holiday, which I had really enjoyed and it had helped to remove the grey cloud which had been hanging over me after Jean died. I would remember her as a charming, loving and humorous woman, which was what she wanted me to do.

Chapter 13
Battling My Conscience

Pushing open my front door with a bigger than usual mound of mail behind it, the house seemed strangely quiet after the hectic and eventful journey across America. My first call was at the local supermarket to restock my fridge and after putting everything away, I settled down to read my mail. There was a letter from Janice in South Wales telling me how sorry she was about her daughter being rude to me and that they were now good friends again. I would be welcome to visit her whenever I had free time from all my activities and she thought the holiday in Egypt was the best she had ever had. Janice seemed keen to get together again, but I had no wish to respond.

I had now seen at first hand the problems with jealous daughters and like Dickie, I was not going to run the risk of unpleasant confrontations. Janice was a lively and very pleasant lady, but I would not be taking up her invitation. I also had two requests to join meetings with local residents hoping to set up their own versions of the Fairfields Garden Club and an invitation to an interview on Radio Leeds. There were also big discounts available on solar panel installations, windows, doors and new kitchens. A short note from Helen told me that she had looked after things in my absence, but knowing that I would be back, had arranged to travel to London to meet up with a retired colleague. By the middle of the afternoon, I had brought my house back to full working order and was ready to join Dickie for our evening meal at The Yorkshireman pub. I ordered a drink from Rod and thanked him for looking after things in my absence. He passed over a bundle of papers Helen had left and since there was no sign of Dickie, I sat down at our usual table to begin going through them. One of our volunteers who had cut the lawn in our garden suggested that we should buy a small trolley to move mowers, in case some members could not get theirs into a car. I thought this was a good idea and put it down for discussion at our next meeting. There were also three requests from residents for help with their house, or garden, which I decided I could do.

I had been sitting for half an hour before Dickie arrived with the latest news about Trudy. She was now settled in at Jean's house and had met with Jean's brother to allow him to collect family and any other items he wanted. Dickie was invited to stay, since Trudy felt lonely living amongst new neighbours and she would like his help with some furniture changes. Her divorce decree had been passed and her husband had offered to give her cash for her half share in the house, but she thought it was worth more than the figure he was using for his offer and was checking on the price he accepted from the buyer. Dickie was returning to York the next day and hoping that Trudy would be more tempted by his invitation to become his partner. I wondered whether this was what she wanted after her unpleasant marriage.

"Trudy now has her independence from her husband and she has her own home. I think she may be more likely to want you to move to York than give up her own home to move in with you, particularly if you are not offering marriage."

Dicky looked startled to hear my views and certainly did not have marriage in mind after his own acrimonious divorce and ongoing difficulties with his ex-wife. At least my comments made him consider likely options before meeting Trudy, but I was sure that he would have difficulty persuading Trudy to accept his idea. We were both feeling tired after our flight and after finishing our meals, headed home for bed. Tomorrow I would do my work with FGC and Dickie would be on his way to stay with Trudy. Life would be very quiet for the next few days with both Helen and Dickie away from the area.

Next morning, I telephoned Mrs D Brewer to ask when I could call to help with her problem shower. After a rather long wait my call was answered and I explained that I was from FGC and would be happy to do what I could to solve her problem.

"Call me Doris, love. I read about you in the paper and I think it is very kind of you to help. Could you drop in about eleven this morning, only I have a hairdressing appointment in the afternoon?"

"Certainly, Doris. Can you tell me what the problem is so that I can bring the right tools?"

"The thing holding my plastic curtain has come loose and I have to hold the shower in my hand now, or the water would go all over the place love."

"Right, I think you mean the bar connecting it to your ceiling has pulled away."

Doris thought that must be the fault and I hoped it would simply need new screw fittings to support the shower curtain and packed my tools and screws in my tool bag. I judged there was ample time to give my car a wash before going to see Doris. At eleven, I was ringing the doorbell and met Doris, who had wet hair and was wearing a dressing gown. She explained that she had not realised the time and was having a shower in case it would take some time before I could fix it. I was shown into the small bathroom and could see the sagging metal shower frame, which had come away from the ceiling.

"Have you got a stepladder, Doris, or perhaps I could use a chair to reach the ceiling?"

Doris went off and returned with a chair. I stepped on the wobbly seat and found that one screw was partly out and there were three holes from screws missing from the frame. After plugging the holes, I asked Doris if she could hold my screwdriver as I pushed the screws through the frame. She stood beside the chair and put one arm around my leg as she held my screwdriver in the other hand. When I turned to reach for it, I found myself looking down at her bare chest and suspected that she was only wearing a dressing gown. Finishing the fitting, I thanked her for her help and told her that she could let me go now so that I could step down. It might just be that I had called when she was in the shower, but I was unhappy about her simply putting on a dressing gown to take an unknown man with her into her bathroom. Doris released me and in doing so gave me an even larger view of her ample bosom. She said I must stay for tea or coffee because she was so grateful that she could now have a proper shower.

"That is really kind of you, Doris, but I have more work to do on the estate and I just had my coffee before coming to see you."

It was a relief to get back to my car and I wondered if I was making unfair judgements about Doris, who might have pressed herself against my leg to prevent me from falling off the chair. Perhaps she had not realised that her dressing gown had opened so wide at the top. Tradesmen may well find themselves doing work in homes where they are alone with the lady owner and may themselves take advantage or may be encouraged by the lady herself. Loneliness or the special thrill of a casual affair with a stranger in the home may lead to out of character behaviour. I went home for lunch and was surprised to receive a phone call from Gloria.

"Hi Tom. Are you missing me, I am certainly missing you?"

"Well, Gloria. What a surprise. It has to be only our second day back and I thought you would be outdoors riding your horse or checking on the takings from your hairdressing business."

"I know nothing about hairdressing, darling. Dorothy trained as a hairdresser and looks after that part and I make sure that the business runs well and makes a profit. Not that we need the money, but it gives us both an interest and we get our hair done for nothing. There is a good show on in the city that my friends are all raving about and I wondered if you would like to come down for the night."

With my busy lifestyle, I wondered if I could spare the time.

"When did you have in mind, Gloria, because I play tennis tomorrow and I am looking after the garden club on my own at the moment?"

"Any night when you are free, my love. I am in your hands, at least I hope so."

"Thursday this week is free, if you can get tickets. I think I know the musical you mean and it is a long time since I last saw a London show. I will probably stay at the Cumberland near Hyde Park."

"Will Dickie be able to come as well, because if Dorothy and I both go up to the evening show, it would not be suspicious if we stayed overnight? Also, would you mind staying at one of the small hotels in Bayswater so that we avoid meeting any of our friends?"

"I am not happy about hiding away in a small Bayswater hotel, which seems rather sordid to me. Dickie has gone to York for a few days and I will have to ring him and hear what he thinks before giving you an answer on this."

Gloria was disappointed but preferred to ring me next morning to find out if the two of us could travel to a London liaison, which made me think that her husband already had his suspicions about his wife and her outings with Dorothy. When I tried to contact Dickie, I was referred to his answer phone and asked him to ring me anytime during the day. Lunch over, I went off to make my second and third visits to residents who needed help from FGC. Both were elderly and at the first, I was able to use the resident's mower to cut the lawn. For the other lady, I had to cut back the bushes partly blocking her entrance path. It was fortunate that at the first call there was a lawn mower, but this might not always be the case and we certainly did need to buy our own mower as well as a heavy cutter and other tools, which I planned to suggest at our meeting in a week's time. After showering and changing my clothes, I strolled down to The Yorkshireman and sat at the bar, since my usual drinking companions were both away. In between serving his customers, I was able to chat with Rod, who was interested to hear about Route 66. He told me that a reporter from Radio Leeds had called to see him and he gave her my phone number and address to contact me on my return. I told him about the invitation and that I was going to call their number. It seemed strange to be eating dinner on my own and I hoped to have my missing friends join me soon, since I suddenly felt lonely.

Next morning, I rang the number given for Radio Leeds and spoke to Tracey Hogan, who had signed the invitation letter. She asked about the garden and was particularly interested in the follow up service we offered local residents after the original estate garden itself was finished. I mentioned the three residents I had helped yesterday and she asked when I could call at the studio for a radio interview. I suggested a day in the following week because I had not yet heard from Dickie about a night in London.

I played in a tennis match that night and when we finished, I was chatting with Linda who had played with me in the mixed doubles when her friend joined us. We had just won against Magda and her partner and she told us that it was close, but we kept up the pressure until we got the winning point. Magda asked me if I liked the Black Dyke brass band and I said I liked all brass bands, but in particular Black Dyke. Magda told me she had two tickets for a concert in Leeds on Saturday, but her friend was ill and had cancelled, so either she needed to find a new companion, or a couple who could make use of both tickets. Linda was attending a birthday dinner and couldn't go, but she suggested that I might be able to use the tickets, or even join Magda. I somehow felt I had been manipulated, but since I expected to be on my own on Saturday night, I gave my best smile and said I would be delighted to join Magda.

Over the years, I had played against Magda quite often and knew she was a Mrs but had never met her husband at any of the regular tennis functions.

"I don't know where you live, Magda, but would you like me to pick you up, or meet at the venue?"

"Parking could be difficult, Tom. I live at Roundhay, but I can easily take the bus in."

"No need, Magda. I will pick you up and there should be plenty of parking spaces on Saturday, since the workers should all be in their homes."

I finally heard from Dickie, who explained that he had accidentally left his phone at home when he drove off to York. He rang on Trudy's phone to tell me that he would be coming back on Saturday, because Trudy was having a visit from her daughter and grandson and he did not want to be there when his arrangement with Trudy was at a sensitive stage. I mentioned the theatre invitation from Gloria and he told me to push the visit into the following week.

"Would you like me to suggest Thursday night in London?"

"That suits me, but I wasn't as lucky with Dorothy as I suspect you were with sexy Gloria, although you have never told me how your two swims went off."

"You know how keen I am on swimming Dickie and Gloria just happened to be just as keen. She is a really good swimmer and was alongside me as I swam every length in the pool."

"She might have been alongside you all right, but somehow I don't think it was in a pool."

"Right leave it with me and I will ask Gloria when she would like us to be in London."

After Dickie rang off, I began to wrestle with my conscience about travelling to London to meet a married woman. Somehow our time together in Las Vegas had seemed acceptable. It was a holiday romance and Gloria had been neglected and I never thought we would ever meet up again, or did I? Travelling to London and hiding in a small Bayswater hotel was quite different. I had already spoken with Gloria twice on the phone and told her that I was still trying to contact Dickie. I would now have to wait until she called again. I was beginning to have doubts about going to London to meet her and postponed making my decision until she next called me. Gloria was a very determined lady and if not me, then she would certainly find someone else for her clandestine affairs. When I woke the following morning, I knew that I would not be accepting Gloria's invitation to a night in London. My conscience was finally overcoming my natural male urges.

I rang my daughter and arranged to call in and see her and my new grandson. As I was putting away my plate and cutlery after breakfast, my doorbell rang and I welcomed Helen back after her visit to London. She seemed quite pleased to see me and was interested in my journey across America. Not only had the break pulled me out of my previous sad mood, it seemed that during my absence Helen had also regained her usual confidence. On impulse, I told her that I was just off to visit my daughter and would she like to come with me to meet my new grandson. Her face lit up and she said she would love to meet them both. My daughters already knew about Jean's tragic death and were sorry that I had lost a very close friend. When we arrived, Karen met us at the door with young Michael in her arms. I introduced Helen to my daughter.

"Morning, love. I can see that Michael is showing the family features with those big blue eyes and fair hair. This is Helen, who is my neighbour and she has worked really hard in setting up our garden club. I know that I could never have done it without her help."

As we stepped inside, Helen was allowed to hold Michael and I told Karen that she had trained as a midwife but was now retired. We shared coffees and Michael was perfectly happy to stay in Helen's arms as I gave Karen more details of the Route 66 tour. Although the baby's name had been chosen, Karen had yet to arrange the christening for Michael at the local church and asked if I was about to go off on any more foreign holidays. I assured her that I expected to be at home for the next month or two, or at the very least until after the christening. Our visit over, Helen returned Michael to his mother, who had welcomed the respite from her twenty-four-hour care of the new baby. I took Helen back to my house and thanked her again for taking care of FGC during my holiday. We also spoke about the three residents I had helped and my experience with the woman in her revealing bathrobe.

"Oh how embarrassing that must have been for you. Was it impossible to look over her shoulders instead?"

"I was perched on a rickety chair and holding up a shower frame with one hand and turned to her to get my screwdriver.

She had a very big chest and it was between me and my screwdriver."

Helen laughed and said she was only winding me up, which I did all the time to other people. Since I was guilty, I could say no more in my defence. I also told her about my intention to raise the purchase of a trolley to carry lawnmowers around the estate. The next FGC meeting was on Sunday and we sent off our e-mail invitations to all our members, with copies to the local councillor and newspaper reporter. The more publicity we got, the more help and funding we were likely to gain. At The Yorkshireman, Helen joined me for an evening meal and although Dickie was still absent, I was very glad to have company again after dining alone for the past few days. We walked back together to our homes and I began to feel that I was settling back into my usual routine after the incredible journey along Route 66.

Just as I was getting ready to go to bed my phone rang and I heard Gloria's voice.

"Hello, my gorgeous lover from the north. Have you found Dickie yet?"

I explained that he was staying with relatives and would not be back for a while, which ruled out a London visit. I also told her that I did not like the idea of hiding away in a London hotel for our meeting. I suspected that Gloria had taken one or two drinks and was probably in her bedroom at this time, judging by the slurred sounds of her voice.

"Ho, ho, lover. If you can't come south, then I will just have to come north. There must be nice hotels with big swimming pools up there, or better still, small beds. I won't take no for an answer. After Las Vegas, I just have to have some fun in my life instead of my boring existence with hubby. Goodnight, my love, be seeing you."

With the phone down, I had no chance to respond. I searched my holiday papers and found Gloria's number, which I thought would be safe to ring if she was in her own bedroom. The phone was switched off, probably deliberately I thought.

Luckily, she did not have my address and if she did come to Leeds, or York, I would have to speak to her at her hotel and make it clear that Las Vegas was a holiday affair, which could not continue. She would have to try another holiday or another man. It was my first experience with a married woman and I was now telling myself that I should have known better.

Fortunately, my satnav guided me to the secluded road where Magda lived in a large stone built semi-detached house in Roundhay, Leeds. I had only ever seen her in tennis shorts and now in her evening clothes I was surprised to see how glamorous she appeared. After settling her in the passenger seat, I drove to the theatre and suggested that she should hop out and go to her seat but give me my ticket so that I could park the car and join her.

"You don't need to do that, Tom. I am perfectly capable of walking back with you."

"I insist. I walk quickly and know the back streets, which would be no good for you with those heels."

Reluctantly, Magda passed me the ticket and went into the theatre. I found space on the top floor of the car park and hurried back to join Magda just ten minutes before the programme began. Fortunately, she was not bothered about drinks in the interval but accepted my offer to get us both ice creams. I often found that by the time I had fought my way to the bar and bought drinks, the interval was almost over. After the concert ended, I wanted to collect the car while she waited at the theatre, but she said I would find difficulty getting near the entrance and it was easier for her to walk with me to the car. When we reached her house in Roundhay, Magda invited me in for coffee and having found her to be a charming companion I accepted. As we sat in her lounge drinking coffee, she told me that she and her husband had worked hard to expand their printing business. It employed twenty people and they had just invested in the latest machinery when her husband died suddenly from a heart attack. Magda ran the business alone for some time and owned the building near Leeds city centre. She received a generous offer for the building and another offer from a competitor for the printing equipment and customer base and accepted both. She always enjoyed playing tennis, but her husband was a workaholic, which is why we had never seen him at functions. She had a son, but he was a geologist and worked abroad for BP. She was anxious to reassure me about our evening at the theatre.

"I know it might have seemed a little contrived when I offered you a ticket to the concert, but I had genuinely been let down by my best friend, who has severe arthritis. I always found you a very honest player. You were scrupulous about line calls, unlike some others who made false claims to take the point. I was sure I could trust you and I thank you for a very pleasant evening. I hope you won't mind if I invite you again if I am abandoned with spare tickets."

I assured Magda that I too had enjoyed myself and would be happy to be her escort if needed. As I said goodnight, I went to take her hand, but she kissed me on the cheek before leading me to her door. As I drove home, I was glad that a long-term tennis acquaintance had now joined my growing circle of good friends.

I presented myself at the Radio Leeds studio and had a brief chat with Tracey Hogan before beginning the short on-air interview. Tracey asked the questions and I tried to give short but clear answers about the idea of turning an eyesore into a garden and then establishing the community service as the Fairfields Garden Club. I expressed my gratitude for the help from rotary, our local councillor and our very generous sponsor, whom I named. Most of all I wanted to thank the local residents who had given their time in the building work and were now helping other residents who were infirm or incapacitated. Tracey asked if other areas had shown interest and I explained how Helen and I had both visited estates, which wanted to try something similar. Tracey told her listeners that if they liked what they heard then they now had someone to contact for advice. She gave out the telephone number of The Yorkshireman pub, which was our headquarters. I had told Rod about the interview in advance and we agreed that although Helen and I were not always available, he was anchored to The Yorkshireman and was available every day and all day to accept phone calls. I sympathised with him but suggested that the free publicity must be a bonus as well as increasing his catering turnover from visitors and hungry FGC workers. He told me that more customers meant more work, but he was happy to help my radio career.

As a result of the interview, there were a number of requests for phone responses from communities who were interested and invitations to attend their meetings. It looked like Helen and I would be having a busy time following them all up. One call came directly to me and it was Diane from Altrincham, who had been my fellow passenger on the flight back from Los Angeles. After asking how I was and had I been busy with the FGC, Diane invited me to join a meeting she was holding to consider matching what we had done. She said that unfortunately it was an evening meeting on Friday, but she would provide accommodation so that I could join everyone with drinks afterwards and avoid crossing The Pennines at night. I agreed to attend and entered the date in my rapidly filling diary.

At the Sunday meeting of FGC, there were sixty people, including almost half who were not yet members. The rotary duo, councillor and reporter were becoming regulars and I suspected that the Radio Leeds broadcast and mention of their support had been a key motivator. My proposal to purchase a trolley was approved and a member suggested we should also buy our own mower. We would then have to find somewhere to store the mower, trolley and any other tools we needed. I was tasked with looking for suitable storage, before purchasing the extra equipment. Our friendly reporter told me that he thought my interview was good and he was trying to get a friend who worked for Leeds TV to feature us in their *Round and About* programme. This was marvellous news and we might yet make a video of Fairfields Garden Club, which could be sent to other communities wanting to set up their own clubs. We could make a charge for the hire of our video, which would initially make up our production cost and then add to our income. Next, I briefly outlined my ideas for extra activities we might add. There was a very positive response, but it was decided that we should first establish a walking club for residents.

Helen joined me for lunch and I told her about the radio interview and possible contact by Leeds TV. I wondered if she would speak about her visit to London, but instead she asked if she had offended me in some way and I was quite surprised to hear this.

"What makes you think you have offended me, Helen?"

"You seem to have distanced yourself from me somehow and now it's all business and no jokes, or your usual thoughtful gestures. You have changed and I wondered at first if it was because of Jean. I thought your holiday would help, but I don't think it has made much difference."

"Helen, imagine looking into a mirror. If you smile, it smiles back and if you frown, you see a frown. You very definitely gave me the impression that you wanted no close contact with me after our night together and I thought it was because you thought I had taken advantage. Since you wanted me to keep my distance, I tried to do just that."

"I never blamed you. I was the one who got into your bed and I know that I have been miserable, but it was because I lost a lifetime friend and realised that after so many years, I still enjoyed a man's company."

"Well then, please treat me as a man and close friend. For heaven's sake, we spend so much time together and you are a very attractive woman. It has been difficult for me to maintain an arm's-length relationship when we spend so much time together, but I thought that was what you wanted."

"I'm sorry. I was confused because I wasn't sure what I wanted, but I do enjoy our time together and having been hurt once, I was afraid of being hurt again and you always seem to have lots of ladies you are friendly with."

"Helen, I was married for many years and only loved and made love to one woman, my wife. I am becoming accustomed to being single again and to my new life style. When I was on holiday with Dickie, I met Jean and we later went on holiday together, but she quite accepted that our night together was part of that change. I don't know if my relationship with Jean would have developed into something stronger if she had lived. Attitudes have changed and now men and women make love because they want to and not only when they are in a permanent relationship. At our age, there are far fewer years remaining to us and I want to make the most of every one of them, but would not want to hurt you, or any other woman by my behaviour."

Before Helen could respond, Dickie arrived and apologised for missing the FGC meeting. As he was about to attend, a very emotional Trudy had rung him because her daughter had told her that as soon as the divorce was granted, her mother had taken a new man into her life after sleeping apart from her father for so long. Trudy was upset that her daughter believed all that her father told her and never mentioned the ladies he invited into his cab, or the other woman in his life. It took an hour-long conversation to calm her down and he was going across to York as soon as he had eaten a late lunch. After quickly gulping down his sandwich and beer, we waved him off for his journey back to York.

I had told Rod that I had something to discuss with him and he asked if we would like more drinks to give him time for the busy bar to clear. I explained my idea to Helen:

"I am wondering if Rod has some space where we could keep FGC tools, or perhaps he has room for a wooden garden shed in his yard. We have a healthy bank account at the moment and could pay rent or even buy a shed. Perhaps we should consider charging a membership subscription, but before that happens, there are other activities we could add to encourage locals to join and be more prepared to pay a subscription. Now that we have approval, we can start by planning the walking group."

Before I could explain what I had in mind, Rod joined us and I told him about my ideas for storing FGC equipment. He told us he had a store cupboard at the back of the premises, which was filled with old wooden crates and junk. I would have to empty it and fit a new lock, but we could use it free of charge until we were ready to pay him rent. Our storage problem was solved and Rod went back to his bar and Helen and I left for home. On the way I received a dinner invitation.

"Would you like to come and have dinner with me tonight and at the same time you can tell me about the other plans you have for FGC? It's just as easy cooking for two as for one."

After our conversation in the pub, I saw this as an olive branch as well as a chance to get her reaction to some of the extra activities I had in mind.

"I would really like that Helen and I would also like to know what you think about the new ideas I have for our FGC."

I was busy writing up my notes on the meeting when my phone rang and I heard Gloria's voice again.

"Hello darling. Guess where I am sitting at the moment."

"Hello Gloria. I have no idea where you are sitting, so why not just tell me."

“I have a room at the Queens Hotel in Leeds and I want you to come and have dinner with me. I am in room 103 and if you check with reception, they will send you straight up to me.”

“Sorry Gloria. I have a meeting with a colleague on our garden project tonight. You should have told me that you were coming to Leeds.”

“If you come over tonight, I will go back to Croydon tomorrow, but if you leave me stranded here on my own, I will just have to come over to where you live tomorrow instead.”

I had never given Gloria my address, but perhaps Dickie had told Dorothy and there was no time to check with him. I was annoyed with myself for not having warned him about doing so, but because he was looking forward to returning home to Trudy, I knew that he had not exchanged phone numbers with Dorothy. Gloria could not have my house address, but perhaps she knew the area where I lived, unless she was bluffing. The only way to end this was to face Gloria and make her stop this unpleasant pursuit. I was a widower, but she had a husband who might react badly to her affair with me.

“All right, Gloria, I should be able to get there by around 6.30 pm, as long as I can contact the organiser first and put back our meeting.”

“That’s wonderful. I knew I could rely on you and can’t wait to see you again. Bye, darling.”

Next, I rang Helen to apologise for having to call off our chat and dinner so that I could meet up with a colleague who was unexpectedly staying in Leeds overnight only. She said that she had not started preparing the meal yet and perhaps I could make it on Monday, which I said would be ideal. Having just begun to restore our previous friendly style, I wanted to hold on to it. I had no intention of staying overnight in Leeds and chose the car for the journey to the city centre, since parking should be no problem on Sunday evening. I anticipated that Gloria would be waiting for me in her hotel room wearing only a dressing gown or even less. I would have to insist that she came down to reception to meet me and we would have dinner together as I made it clear that our holiday affair was ended.

The young lady at reception told me that Miss Hammond was waiting for me and directed me to the lift. I explained that I was pressed for time and since we would probably be dining in the hotel restaurant, would Miss Hammond come down and meet me in reception. The receptionist called Room 103 to pass on my message, but after a brief conversation she then gave the phone to me at Miss Hammond's request.

"I expected to meet you in my room darling and not in reception. You could hardly wait to get into my room when we were in Las Vegas."

With the receptionist listening to my conversation, I made my reply as bland as possible.

"Yes. I am really sorry to be in such a rush, but I do hope you can come down for dinner at least before I have to hurry off."

Gloria slammed down the phone on me and after giving the receptionist my best smile, I told her that it was a surprise visit by Miss Hammond and unfortunately it clashed with a later meeting I had arranged. She did not appear to be convinced. After waiting for half an hour, Gloria appeared in an obviously expensive dress and after giving me a big smile and kiss on the cheek, she took my arm as we walked to the dining room. Taking the waiter's arm, Gloria asked him to find us a corner table, which was not difficult since the restaurant was barely half full. Before I had picked up the menu, Gloria wanted to know why I had embarrassed her by not going to her room as arranged.

"It was your request and not an arrangement. Las Vegas was special because of the unique atmosphere and being together for two weeks. Holidays are just make-believe, where there is no daily work and nights are spent in luxury hotels with new experiences and attractions to entertain us throughout the day. When the holiday ends, we go back to reality in our normal environment. We, neither of us expected or intended that it should be anything other than a holiday romance, which you told me you were looking for."

"I thought it was, but when I got back to my dreary life with my zombie husband, I knew that I had fallen in love with you. Since I got back from America, all I can think about is our time together in my room and in the shower and the pool. After Las Vegas, I realised that my world has changed and I don't want my old miserable life back again."

Gloria reached across the table and took hold of my hand as she looked at me, but I was determined not to be tempted again.

"You fell in love with make believe, Gloria, and now you want to put the clock back to Las Vegas by having me come to London and hide in a hotel to avoid making your husband suspicious. We live very different lives and there is no way they can mix."

"I don't care what my husband thinks, or does anymore. At his age, I know that as long as I am discreet, he will pretend it isn't happening and he would certainly never divorce me. If he did, he would end up living alone and I would have a very big cash settlement and be free to do as I please. I only have to wait and I will eventually get all his money, since he has no children or relatives."

"Fine, so you can do as you please, but so can I. The American holiday was intended to help me to get over the sudden death of a close friend and I thank you for being a big part of that. Perhaps, from what you have just told me, I may have helped you to break out of a very dull and passionless lifestyle. Your home, your friends and everything you are familiar with is in Croydon and mine is here and I am not going to change it."

The waiter came to take our order and we had to end our dialogue as we quickly made our choice from the menu. Gloria wanted to order a bottle of wine, but I told her that I was driving and only wanted a small glass. Gloria still ordered a full-sized bottle. The wine came first and I made sure I did not touch my filled glass, because I expected Gloria to keep topping it up. It would then be unsafe for me to drive home and I would have to stay the night. We finished our meal and ordered coffee to be brought to us in the lounge, which to my surprise was empty, apart from us. Putting her hand over mine Gloria tried her best to convince me to stay.

"You really are determined not to spend the night with me, aren't you? I came all this way just to be with you and you are here now. Why not make it our last night together and in the morning, we can go our separate ways?"

"Gloria, it ended when we left Las Vegas, so let's just keep our memories, but accept that."

I finished my coffee and stood. Gloria came up to me, put her arms around me and asked for a last kiss. She held on to me and our bodies were pressed tightly together, with Gloria's tongue flicking into my mouth. Finally, I gently took her arms away and said goodbye, which made her face red with anger.

"You bastard. I only have to lift a finger and men rush to do what I want. What makes you think that you are so special that after coming all this way, you are walking away because you have suddenly developed a conscience?"

Her eyes were blazing with anger and for a moment I was tempted to try to justify my behaviour, but common sense prevailed and I turned and hurried from the lounge to get to my car. My mind was still busy turning over our meeting as I drove and I was surprised to find my car had reached my drive, although I could not remember making the journey. I had left my drink untouched at the dinner table and now poured myself a brandy to go with my coffee as yet again I reviewed the evening with Gloria. It was well past midnight when I got to bed. I tried and failed to close down my mind and get to sleep but kept reliving Las Vegas and the Queens Hotel over and over. I finally gave up and showered before having a very early breakfast and then walking to the store for a paper and hoping the two-mile return journey would freshen me up.

Just after 10 am next morning, I was surprised to receive a visit from Helen.

"After you rushed off to meet your friend, when I finished my meal, I walked down to the pub and had a drink with Rod, in between his bar work. I was walking back when I saw you in your car and waved, but you drove straight on. Was it a difficult meeting with your friend, because you certainly did not look very happy?"

"Yes, it was a pain and I had to hear about all the problems in the marriage before I could offer my advice, which hopefully was accepted. We had a meal together and I couldn't wait to get back home to bed."

Helen looked a little puzzled by my explanation and I felt guilty about only giving her such very brief details. I hoped that I had now ended relations with Gloria and there was no need to say any more. However, knowing how determined and angry she was at being rejected, I still felt concern that she might continue to harass me.

Chapter 14
New Ideas

After going over my ideas for expanding the FGC by adding new services and new members, Helen agreed that we should talk them over with Rod, since we needed The Yorkshireman pub as our regular monthly meeting place. As usual, he was always ready to consider anything which brought business to his pub and was prepared to help as much as possible.

"I have three ideas in mind, Rod. First, I would like to add a regular walking group to the club, which would arrange its own monthly walks around the area, but possibly start with a walk along the Leeds canal. Another addition would be a baby or child-sitting service with mature residents, or couples providing an evening, or even day sitting service. Young couples with babies need a break, but reliable baby sitters are hard to find. Light refreshments would have to be provided for the sitters. We have quite a few retired or single residents on the estate who might enjoy helping young families needing a reliable sitter. We could also start an investment club for those willing to stake a monthly sum to be included in the club investments chosen by members. The invested total should grow and members would be able to increase their monthly stake, or withdraw their accumulated share if they needed it, or if they leave the club. All three would meet monthly here in your pub, but not necessarily on the same night."

Rod listened and I watched as his eyebrows rose at times, but he also nodded his head.

"That is quite a list, Tom. Are you planning to launch them at the next meeting?"

"Talk about them, yes, but it would be better to take one at a time and I would then ask for a vote on which order we should introduce them. If we put details on the monthly e-mail circular, with a request to residents to respond on which they want to become involved with, we can begin setting them up. It would have to be one at a time of course."

"Perhaps I should have a little sign made to show that my pub is also the FGC centre."

"Fine by me, Rod, and it could well bring in even more customers."

Rod had work to do, but before leaving us, he passed me a note about a resident who had asked if anyone could help with his garden, because he was crippled with arthritis. Helen smiled at me and said it was definitely a job for a man. She went shopping and I returned home and telephoned Albert before driving to his house. My guess was that he was in his seventies and I could see that his hands were badly twisted and judging by his difficulty walking, his knees were also affected. He lived alone after the death of his wife and relied on his daughter for help with anything beyond his limited abilities. His garden was very overgrown with the usual mix of tall grass and weeds, but no sign of discarded rubbish. In his garden shed, he had all the tools needed and I calculated that it would take me a full day to dig out and bag the weeds before I would be able to rake over the soil. If it was seeded to make a lawn, it would require regular cutting. The maintenance-free alternative was to lay a plastic liner and cover the surface with gravel, which would be a big job for me to take on alone. Albert was quite happy for me to come whenever I liked to do the work, since he rarely left the house and would welcome my company. I had always enjoyed working in my large garden and my current small outdoor area was maintenance free, but undemanding.

During the afternoon, Diane rang me to confirm arrangements for Friday and told me how much her group was looking forward to meeting me. The meeting was to be held at the Cresta Court Hotel, which I knew was near the main road through Altrincham. It made a change from the usual church halls, or pub bars where I had attended other meetings. I went over the meeting notes and sent off the FGC news to resident members by e-mail. I was at Helen's door at 5 pm as requested for dinner. She usually wore trousers for meetings and work parties, but she called me in wearing a bright flower pattern blouse and grey skirt. There was no doubt in my mind that tonight she wanted me to see her as a woman and I had never seen her looking so attractive. The table was set and a bottle of Shiraz wine was opened. Helen asked me to sit down at the table before going to her kitchen. The main course was lasagne, which was a favourite of mine and I wondered if Helen had remembered me regularly ordering the Italian meal at The Yorkshireman. I supposed that I must just be a creature of habit.

The lasagne was really delicious and I complimented Helen.

"The last time I had a meal in your house it was when you served Dickie and I a salad and I had no idea that you were such a talented cook."

Helen blushed and smiled at my delight with her cooking.

"After a long career in nursing, I was ready for a change from bland cafeteria meals, or very often, no meals at all. Once I had retired and found myself with lots of free time, I booked myself on a Cordon Bleu cooking course. I rarely have a chance to find a victim to practice my cooking skills on. You know yourself that living on your own you tend to go for quick and simple meals."

"Helen, whenever you want to try out your cooking, just remember I am only two minutes' walk away. I know I am an appalling cook and can only just manage to use the microwave, so if you have time to give me some guidance or try out your cooking, I would really appreciate it."

Helen said she would be happy to give me advice on cooking, but with all the schemes and activities I was involved in, she doubted that I would find the time. Enjoying the food and the conversation, I kept sipping away at my wine and was surprised to see Helen open another bottle. When we finished eating, I helped Helen to clear away the dishes and picked up a cloth to help with the washing up but was sent into the lounge while Helen finished off and made the coffee. I sank into a very comfortable chair and felt blissfully relaxed as the wine and a full tummy took effect, as well as my sleepless night. I woke up in darkness and took off the blanket Helen must have put over me after I disgraced myself by falling asleep at my first dinner in her home. Checking my watch, I saw that it was 6 am and I made my way to the front door and opened and closed it as quietly as possible to avoid making things worse by waking Helen.

I had a very early breakfast and did some work on plans for the new FGC developments until just after 9 am when I telephoned Albert, who welcomed me to make a start on battling the weeds in his back garden. He was a regular tea drinker and called me in for a break and a chat three times during the morning before inviting me to join him for lunch. Seeing photographs on the wall of a man in an army uniform, I asked Albert about them and he told me that they were taken when he was a lot younger. He had been a regular in the Army and rose to the rank of warrant officer in REME, which is responsible for maintaining the weaponry, tanks and aircraft in top working order. During his long career, he had also worked on bomb disposal, but now due to his arthritis, he could not even wire a plug for his electric kettle. After washing most of the dirt off, I left with a promise to return on Thursday morning to do battle with the rest of the weeds and place them in bags for the council tip.

Before going off to play tennis, I slipped a note through Helen's letterbox with my apologies for sleeping in her incredibly comfortable chair after enjoying her superb cooking. There had been no answer when I knocked and I hoped I would catch up with her the next afternoon. I also rang Dickie, who told me that he would be coming back from York on Friday. He asked about London.

"Have you got back to your London girlfriend about meeting them yet?"

"I have and told her that there would be no London or any other meetings. She was not happy and on Sunday, she rang me from the Queens hotel in Leeds and threatened me unless

I met her. I went to Leeds and we had dinner and then I left her as mad as hell after making it clear that there was no place for her in my life."

"Good for you. She was always the lively one in that pair. Me and Trudy are getting on really well now and I was never very happy with that Dorothy. It was a good holiday and they were good company, but we are not on holiday any more. See you on Friday."

After he rang off, I remembered that I would be in Altrincham on Friday. I had been doing research on the Leeds and Liverpool Canal, which was 127 miles long and could be ideal for beginning the FGC Walking Group. It could be divided into one-day walks of roughly eight miles, with a packed lunch, or a meal at a pub near the canal. I would try an eight-mile walk on Wednesday by starting at Leeds Dock in the city centre and see for myself how long it took. I also hoped to find a suitable location for our walkers' lunch. On Wednesday morning, I started out from Leeds Wharf with my haversack packed with a waterproof, water bottle, phone and sandwiches for my canal walk. The first part took me alongside the Aire and Calder Canal and River Aire, before moving away from the waterway to pass through city streets and then return to the canal to reach Granary Wharf. I knew Leeds well, but the walk took me to areas which I never knew existed and I seemed to have walked into another world. Normally my longest walk was eighteen holes on a golf course, with regular stops to hit the ball and more stops to try and find it. Now my legs kept moving as I passed buildings and crossed bridges until I saw by my watch that I had been walking for over two hours without a stop. The path was flat and reasonably even so that it was easy to maintain a good pace with very little effort.

I reached Thornhill Bridge and instead of walking under it, I walked across it until I came to a small pub with a sign outside advertising home cooking. My feet and legs were fine and I was pleased with myself and relieved that the morning remained sunny. With no shelter, walkers would have to make sure they carried good rainwear, particularly if the walks continued through the winter. The publican was not over busy and was impressed when I told him that I was on my way to Saltaire as a trial test for a local walking group. He offered to provide a special meal for walkers if the route was chosen and warned me that I had at least another four miles ahead of me to Saltaire. I went back over the bridge and continued on my way at a brisk pace, with regular sniff tests from dogs with their owners giving them walkies along the canal. I usually stood still to avoid provoking them, unless of course I saw them raise one leg. A big portion of the country's Mallard ducks must live on the canals and my brisk pace alarmed them so that they abandoned the toll path and skidded into the water ahead of me. When I met up with the much larger Canada Geese, I had to walk around them since they made no move to give me space. I have been chased by geese and dogs when walking past farms and regretted not having a walking stick to defend myself.

The walk was enjoyable apart from one persistent hazard, the cyclists. My first intimation that there was a cyclist was when the bike flashed past me on what at times was a narrow path beside the canal. I could see and avoid those cyclists coming towards me, but those from behind made no effort to slow their pace and very rarely used their bells, if they had them. There were puddles and dog droppings on the path and if I moved sideways around them as a cyclist passed, I could be injured or the cyclist and I could both end up in the canal. It took me almost two hours before I saw the bulk of the enormous Salts Mill building ahead and once inside, I climbed the stone stairway to reach the restaurant. They had just finished serving lunch and did not provide dinners, but I sat down with a coffee from the espresso bar and wrote up my notes for the walking group. I had once been a member of a Moor and Fell group and walked over the moors through almost knee-high heather, which made walking very strenuous. Our average walk covered twelve miles as we climbed up and down hills, which was probably why I found it so undemanding to walk along the flat path beside the canal. There was no danger from cyclists on the moors, but we were always wary of cows. Over the past fifteen years, more than seventy people had been killed by cows and many more were injured. They can be particularly aggressive when you are accompanied by a dog. It would be best to have a fairly easy walk to start the FGC walking group and from the Leeds Wharf start to Thornhill Bridge should be about right. The group could then end with lunch at the pub I had found. To avoid problems with cyclists I would have white cloth tabards made with 'RING YOUR BELL' printed on the back in bold red letters.

Before leaving Salts Mill, I walked around the extensive bookshop, clothing, home store and art gallery, where David Hockney's paintings are displayed. I would have liked to explore the village built by Sir Titus Salt for his workers in the nineteenth century, but after sitting down for coffee, my legs were beginning to stiffen after the long walk. As I made my way to the railway station for my train back to Leeds, I found an Indian restaurant with a very tempting menu and went inside to take full advantage of my taste for spicy food. I finally arrived home just after 8 pm and wrote down more details on my plan for the first walk while my own experience was fresh in my mind. There was no message from Helen or Dickie and I assumed they were both busy with their own affairs. I sat down in an easy chair with my beer and fell asleep. It was almost midnight when I opened my eyes and I was getting concerned about again having fallen asleep in a chair. Obviously, it was the long walk and nothing to do with my age. I went to bed, since I was due back in Albert's garden in the morning.

Working in Albert's garden, I felt pain from my leg muscles every time I reached down to pull out a weed root and drop it in my plastic bag. By Albert's mid-morning tea break, I was loosening up and learning to live with the pain. It never pays to push your muscles too far and instead the process should be a gradual build up to allow the body to adapt to the new demands. I asked Albert if he would agree to having his garden covered in gravel and he nodded his head.

"My wife loved her flowers and the garden once had a lawn with all sorts of flowers growing around it. After she died, I managed to keep the lawn cut, but I never was much of a gardener and the weeds just took over. Then when my hands got bad, I couldn't even cut the lawn, so looking at gravel is better than looking at those weeds you put in your bags. My wife grew orchids after the garden got too much for her and they don't need much work."

Albert took me into the spare bedroom and I was amazed to see dozens of different coloured flowers blooming on shelves around the room. He showed me the strange stalks growing from the main stem and explained that they were air roots, which drew moisture from the atmosphere and he only needed to apply a little liquid food and water once every two, or three weeks. When he stood in the room surrounded by her orchids, he told me it was almost as if his wife was still there. I left and thought what a wonderful marriage it must have been.

I promised Albert that we would finish the work as soon as we could and it would have to be soon to stop more weeds blowing in and taking over again. At The Yorkshireman that evening, I told Rod about my walk to Salts Mill.

"You must be bloody mad. Salts Mill must be all of thirteen miles and you are no spring chicken."

"You are quite right, Rod, I am and my leg muscles are still telling me I am. I will suggest we do eight-mile maximum walks to avoid putting people off. Going past the buildings with the trees and the ducks should make it a very pleasant walk for most people. We might even take some in wheelchairs, but only until they are ready to call a halt and take a train back."

Rod agreed and thought the possibility of allowing those in wheelchairs would widen the appeal for the club, provided the route was flat and even. I told him that Dickie was in York and he was not surprised.

"Dickie seems to be very keen on the lady in York, but from what he told me, she has her own house and family there. He doesn't want to move in with her in York and is trying to persuade her to move over here, but I don't give much for his chances."

I told him that I had not seen Helen since Monday and Rod explained that she had booked herself on some sort of course down in Eastbourne and had told him she would be driving off early on Tuesday morning to beat the traffic. When I woke up at 6 am in her chair, I thought she was still in bed, but she must have been careful not to wake me up as she left in her car. I wondered what sort of course it could be. Rod had no idea when she was going to come back. Traffic on the M62 on Friday afternoon is normally heavy and I wanted to avoid being late for my meeting in Altrincham. I left late morning on Friday and after a light lunch in a town centre pub in Altrincham, I wandered around the streets until it was nearly time for the meeting at the hotel. Fortunately, the car park had spaces and I was having a coffee in the lounge when I was joined by Diane and her friend Elaine.

We spoke about current activities in FGC and the additional services being planned. Both ladies were very active in the women's institute and were hoping to broaden their activities by getting members involved in community services. They were interested in setting up a garden club and possibly add a walking group and investment club later, but did not want to become involved in babysitting. They hoped to have an audience of around thirty for tonight and asked if I would follow their general meeting by describing how the FGC began and our current activities. Diane told me that her house was currently being decorated, but Elaine had plenty of room and would welcome my company for the night. I hoped that this included a separate bedroom after my confrontation with Gloria. I sat at the back of the room and as the meeting began, a lady hurried in and took her seat at the back. I wondered if she had paid a late visit to the toilet and when hastily pulling up her knickers had caught some of her dress in the elastic. As a result, her dress had risen up and she was showing rather a lot of her bare rear. I could hardly warn her, but if I mentioned it to Elaine, the lady could be spared embarrassment.

The WI discussions took an hour and I was then introduced with a mention of my recent interview on Radio Leeds. As I sat down and Diane was making the introductions, I told Elaine about the problem one of her guests had and she thanked me and said she would speak to her. Including Diane and Elaine, there were in total twenty-six very smartly dressed ladies in the audience and I could understand their reluctance to babysitting. I also wondered about their enthusiasm for digging gardens and showed them some before and after photographs of the wild patch of land on our estate before we converted it to an attractive garden. I described our difficulty in digging out deep-rooted weeds, stones and rubbish. To my surprise, they still showed most interest in gardening and walking. There were a number of neglected local areas which the ladies thought could be made into attractive gardens. There was also the Bridgewater Canal as the main route through the area and both trams and trains to the start, or return, giving ample scope for walks. The meeting ended and Elaine warned the woman about her dress problem, who blushed, adjusted her dress and waved her thanks to me. The drinks in the bar involved only Diane and Elaine, instead of with all the ladies as I had expected and I assumed it was to give the two ladies more time to question me about the FGC, or at least I hoped it was. Diane asked me if I had taken up any hobbies since retiring and I told her that I had always wanted to try painting watercolours and received a box of paints amongst my retirement gifts. She wanted to know more.

"I hope you have made good use of your paints."

"My wife died and since then I have been too busy changing my life to get down to painting, but I may try them one day."

Diane told me that she had been painting for years and had booked a five-day painting course in Scotland, but the decorators changed their dates and she would now be unable to go. The course was due to start on Sunday and her money would be wasted, unless she could transfer the course to someone. Would I like to finally try out the paints by going in her place?

I tried to refuse by claiming that there was no time to rearrange my affairs, but Diane pointed out that I lived alone and was retired. She refused to take no for an answer. Helen was already away; my paints had been gathering dust for three years and I would only be there five days. I finally agreed, but insisted that I must pay the cost. Diane would not accept because I was doing her a favour by not wasting her place on the course. She arranged to drop off the holiday booking documents at Elaine's house in the morning. We said goodnight and I followed Elaine to her house in my car. The house was large and detached with ample parking space on the drive. As we entered, two very small, very noisy dogs began jumping up and down on Elaine and she explained that they were like family and kept her company. She led me upstairs to my bedroom, which had an en suite bathroom and a large bay window facing the front garden. Elaine asked me to go into her lounge for coffee and a chat after I had settled in. As I sat down, two furry bundles leaped on to my knees and began their noisy yapping as they tried to lick my hands and face. My expression must have shown my annoyance, because Elaine immediately walked them out to their baskets in her kitchen and apologised.

"Sorry. I don't often have visitors and they just want to be friendly, but it makes conversation and drinking coffee difficult."

Elaine had been a qualified solicitor, but after her husband died, she retired to become involved in her local community and was now a local councillor. Diane was embarrassed when she could not find room for me and assured Elaine that after chatting for hours on the flight from Los Angeles, I could be trusted. She had also reached the same conclusion as we three had drinks together in the hotel, which was why they kept me to themselves. I was offered brandy to go with the coffee and Elaine said that the house was far too big for her and it was a pleasure to have company, if only for one night. She had considered moving to an apartment, but without a garden, she would have to give up her dogs. Diane had told her about my tour along Route 66 and was trying to persuade her to join her on the holiday. She had spent time in New York and really liked America, but would have to put her dogs in a home for two weeks. She listened as I filled in more details and decided that it would be an adventure they should both enjoy. We were having breakfast together when Diane arrived with the holiday documents. Elaine told her we had discussed Route 66.

"Tom took me through his Chicago start to the Los Angeles finish and is a very good salesman. I think it would be an interesting holiday we should both enjoy."

Diane thanked me for convincing her friend to join her and told me it was a fair exchange for the painting holiday. When it was time to leave, both ladies kissed me and Elaine urged me to come and stay, particularly for a future visit to the Tatton Park Flower Show. With a gleam in her eye, she assured me that the invitation was also open to the lady who worked with me in my garden club. As I drove back across The Pennines, I was surprised that I had said so much about Helen that it led Elaine to assume that we were very close friends. After crashing out after the dinner, I wondered what sort of reception I could expect when we met again after our separate courses.

My Saturday was filled with preparations for the long drive to Scotland and finding my paints, easel and folding chair for likely outdoor sessions. After thinking about painting for so many years, but never finding the time, I was now looking forward to the holiday. In the evening, I met Dickie in The Yorkshireman and we had dinner together. He described how Trudy now saw him as her champion after the divorce from her adulterous husband. They were, however, not yet discussing where they might live together, since Trudy was still enjoying the pleasure of having her own home and the security with the money left to her in Jean's will. I thought it was a good time to test his thinking.

"Have you thought what you will do if Trudy refuses to move from her house to live with you here?"

"Yes, and if I have to choose between keeping Trudy by moving to York, or losing her by remaining here, I might have to move."

"York is not that far. If you both stay in your own homes, you could still meet whenever you want. It might make your times together that more special."

"I am getting older and know I would enjoy having Trudy looking after me and I want to look after her and do all the jobs around the house that she can't do. After the honeymoon years, my marriage was a disaster, but with Trudy, I think it would really work. We never know how much time we have left."

He was surprised to hear that I was off to Aberdeen in the morning, with a 4 am start for my drive to the university. The accommodation was being provided in the students' residence during the summer vacation period. I expected to be back late afternoon on Friday, since there should be no weather holdups at this time of year. If Dickie decided to move to York, I would lose my fellow holiday traveller, but we should still be able to meet occasionally for clay shooting. For the past few months, he had been spending much of his time at York and with my involvement in FGC, we had seen far less of each other than usual. If he did move to York to live with Trudy, I would have to find myself another travel and shooting companion.

The university was on the outskirts of Aberdeen and my room had its own bathroom and was small but comfortable. I met the other painters and our instructor over dinner and we were only nineteen in total, mainly ladies as usual. Perhaps climbing, walking and potholing were bigger holiday attractions for men or match of the day on TV. Our instructor, or 'Call me Jennie' was in her late fifties and what I would call a 'Jolly hockey sticks lady', who charged around and gave us all a hearty handshake and promise that by the end of the course we would be turning out quality watercolours.

Our first day was spent in the classroom as we experimented with mixing our own colours, using cotton wool balls on wet blue coloured areas to make fluffy white clouds and sprinkling salt on wet paint to create pitted surfaces such as sandy beaches. After dinner, Jennie invited me to join her for table tennis and I had to play hard to match her attacking style. There were other courses also using university buildings and a disco dance was in full swing when I walked into the central hall. As there was a shortage of men, most of the couples on the floor were ladies and Jennie interrupted my people-watching to take me onto the dance floor. Half way through the dance, I was surprised to have another lady interrupt to dance with me. My new partner was from London on a singles' holiday tour in Scotland and thought that all the dancers were on similar holidays. She was surprised that mine was for painting but checked that I was also single and that I had travelled by car. Over the next few days, I became accustomed to Sue appearing beside me whenever we were enjoying free time after our organised daily activities.

Our second day was spent at Crathes Castle, Banchory and we all set up our easels and chairs where we thought it would be the best location to paint the castle. There were round turrets and spires and the walls were a mixed colour as the result of moss and weathering over the centuries. I had difficulty matching the unusual colour effect and making the turrets look round instead of flat. After my initial sketching, I concentrated on getting the perspective right on two adjoining turrets and began to have the feeling I was being watched. When I glanced behind me, I saw that I was. There were at least a dozen young Japanese lady tourists standing quietly behind me and looking at my painting. When I smiled at them, they bowed and wished me good morning before returning my smile and pointing at my painting. They were saying something in Japanese before moving on and I could only assume that they stopped to admire the painting on my easel and were paying me compliments. With my paintbrush poised dramatically, I watched as they walked off to try and find another castle painting to compare with mine. Jennie walked around to check on her pupils and give advice, before calling us in for lunch at the castle. Our coach then took us back to the campus so that we could put the finishing touches on our masterpieces in the classroom. I have never been back to Crathes Castle but hope to return one day to walk through the wonderful gardens and grounds and watch the herons and buzzards near the lake and nature trail. After an hour in the classroom, my painting of Crathes Castle was finished and I proudly signed my work and gave it to Jennie. It would be exhibited with the other paintings for all the holiday guests to consider and award points. The three best paintings would then receive prizes.

There was still time before dinner and I went to the putting green to enjoy the sun and help to improve my putting. Starting at six feet, I began experimenting with longer puts from different spots on the green. Once again, I had the feeling of being watched and when I looked behind me, I found myself looking at a smiling and very friendly Sue. Putting needs concentration and as Sue followed me around the green and bombarded me with questions, my accuracy suffered and I had to give up. She had watched me play table tennis and asked if I wanted a game. What I really wanted was to simply enjoy my own company, but not wanting to be rude or hurt her feelings, I said I had to make some phone calls. I smiled and gritted my teeth when she said she would see me at dinner. The nearest restaurant was about eight miles away, but it might be worth the drive to eat in peace, since Sue was obviously determined to become my companion.

I changed my clothes and was walking to my car when Jennie caught up with me and asked if the course was so bad that I was already going home. I assured her that this was not the case.

"Not at all, Jennie. I am really enjoying it and learning quite a few painting techniques. I just fancied an Italian or Indian dinner."

"What a great idea. This is my third course and I am getting really tired of the same meals every week. Would you mind if I joined you?"

I had become a teacher's pet when learning Spanish and now it looked as if it was happening again with painting. I could hardly refuse and opened the passenger door for Jennie as I said she was welcome. The restaurant was Italian and Jennie was relieved because she told me as we sat at a table that she was not too fond of Indian food. There was a candle in an old wine bottle on our table to create a pleasant atmosphere and the food was good, washed down by a bottle of Chianti.

"Well, Jennie, you are now on your third course and how many are you expecting to complete?"

"It depends on course bookings. We need at least fifteen to make a course viable and this year, with an average of twenty people per course, there are eight courses. I stay here for the whole time because I live in Somerset and it is too far to drive home for weekends. My husband is retired, but we have a smallholding and he looks after the animals while I earn the extra money to buy us a holiday or help to balance the budget."

Jennie was good company and helped by the wine, we chatted away and were both in good spirits as we returned to the university. My room was on the first floor and Jennie's was on the ground floor. The stairs were near the entrance and Jennie said her room was alongside, as I stopped to say goodnight. Jennie smiled before kissing me but made no move to go to her room and seemed to be waiting for me to say, or do something. I told her I had enjoyed our evening and hurried up the stairs. As I lay in my single bed and thought about my day, I wondered whether I had just received an invitation from Jennie, who perhaps was lonely during her stay away from home. After my involvement with Gloria, I was determined to avoid any similar temptations but did find myself attracted to Jennie Hockeysticks, as I thought about her energetic and cheerful approach to life. Still, we could always play more table tennis.

Before entering the restaurant for breakfast, I checked the room first to be sure that Sue was not present and sat down in the corner to eat my food. Within minutes, Sue appeared and sat down beside me before asking where I was last night.

"I went to an Italian restaurant with a friend from my painting course."

"I looked everywhere for you in the restaurant and wondered if you were ill or something and you weren't at the dance either."

"We took our time over the meal and with the wine and after our busy day out painting, I came back and went straight to bed."

Sue looked at me and her expression showed her doubt about my answer, but I made sure that my face had a very innocent look. Checking my watch, I told her it was time to report to the classroom to collect my materials for another painting expedition. She was only half way through eating her porridge and I watched as she considered following me or finishing her porridge. Fortunately for me, the porridge won.

The coach dropped us off at a small harbour on the coast, with a stone breakwater to shelter it from the sea and a number of boats were moored inside. Most of us chose positions on the hill above the harbour, so that we could if we wished, paint a broad view. Other students went down to the breakwater to paint close ups of the boats at their moorings. I sketched out my copy of the view below and began filling in with paints. The tide was out and the boats were mostly tilted over and incredibly difficult to paint with having to show the curved sides and inside view. To avoid painting in the unattractive mixed mud and sand areas left by the receding tide, I moved the sea back in again for my painting. This is allowed for painters under training. Two hours later, I was just putting the finishing touches on my work, when one of my fishing boats suddenly melted as a large Scottish raindrop struck it. I quickly put my jacket over my easel and carried my equipment back to the coach as quickly as possible. It was not so far away, but the shower still left me soaked to the skin. Those painters on the breakwater had to walk up hill and over a longer distance. Jenny was very sympathetic with us and said we would return to the university to dry out and get changed, have a late lunch and then work in the classroom for the rest of the day.

As I was getting off the coach at the university, Jennie grabbed my arm and pulled me to one side before whispering in my ear:

"What about an Italian meal tonight. Dinner is on me?"

Thinking about Sue waiting to pursue me, I agreed and the iron grip on my arm relaxed and I hurried to my room to shower and put on dry clothes. We all worked on our paintings in the security of our classroom and I was able to repair my fishing boat, but many of my fellow students had not been fast enough in covering their work and were forced to start again. Looking at the new painting by the lady on my left, I was very impressed and it made mine look very uninteresting. She had obviously benefitted by having a second attempt and perhaps at the age of eighty-five, she worked better away from damp and windswept Scottish hillsides.

I had made enquiries about any underground tunnels leading from the classroom to my accommodation block in an attempt to evade Sue but was out of luck. I would just have to hurry across open space again to reach sanctuary. Jennie agreed that I could leave all my painting equipment and materials in the classroom. I jogged around to the rear entrance to the block and entered by the back door before hurrying up the stairs to descend on my room from above and avoid being ambushed by Sue. I opened my door and checked to be sure that Sue hadn't somehow found the number and broken in. I could not believe that she was making me so paranoid to avoid her.

I telephoned Jennie to ask her to meet me on the far side of the car park where I had left my car. When she arrived, I was sitting slumped down in my seat to make a low profile. When she asked me why I was doing this, I told her I was just catching up on my sleep and she took me seriously.

"You are not getting enough exercise to help you to sleep. We must have another game of table tennis when we get back."

As long as it was only table tennis she had in mind, it would be fine by me, but she kept bumping into me and putting her face close to mine during the meal. Perhaps her husband had been spending too much time with the animals and not enough time with Jennie. The summer long stay for the painting courses could have stimulated her need for close encounters of the male kind. When we returned to the university grounds, I immediately steered Jennie towards the sports hall to play table tennis. There were two tables and one was in use by four players, one of whom was Sue.

As Jennie and I moved towards the empty table, Sue said she wanted to play us and pulled her male partner over to our table. He was very tall and very thin and I was fascinated by his prominent Adam's apple. Sue introduced him as George from Preston and we began to play. Because of his long reach, George was able to return most of the balls landing at the sides of the table, but had difficulty returning them when they bounced immediately in front of him. I told Jennie about his weak spot and we concentrated our serves and returns to take advantage. Sue had relied on George's ability to return most balls and suddenly found she was exposed to smashes from Jennie and from me. We won by a good margin and George reached down to shake my hand.

Sue tried hard to persuade me to join her at the evening dance, but I insisted that after a day on a rain swept Scottish hillside and a filling Italian meal and wine, I was ready for bed. Jennie had agreed to play another game and I thought it was an ideal time to escape from both ladies and hurried off to sanctuary. Next day, we were taken to a manor house with extensive grounds and magnificent oak trees, plus a river crossed by a hump backed stone bridge. Our painting group split into oak trees, or river bridge painters and I went for the bridge. Having had difficulty matching the weathered stone colours on Crathes Castle, I moved down stream so that the bridge stonework was not quite as detailed and concentrated on getting the variety and colour of the trees and riverbed as realistic as possible. Another student painter set up his easel nearby but soon decided it was the wrong location and moved further away under the trees to gain a better view of the stone bridge. Half an hour later, I heard shouts of fury from him and asked what the problem was.

"Those damned magpies were chattering away in the trees above me and now one of them has fouled my painting and ruined it. Bloody magpies."

Thank goodness I had avoided the trees. It didn't rain and we enjoyed our lunch in the magnificent dining room of the mansion before returning to finish our paintings in the classroom. As I left to return to my room, I was met by Sue, who was waiting for me at the door. Not wanting to be rude, I decided instead to invite her for a coffee to find out why she was so determined to pursue me.

She told me that she had been in a relationship for ten years but earned most of the money because her partner had trouble keeping a job and at times was violent to her. He also had a gambling problem and after their flat in London was repossessed, she left him and returned to live with her parents, who had been warning her for years that he was a loser. All her friends were married and in desperation, she booked a singles' holiday, hoping to find someone with whom she could start her life again. When she met her fellow singles, she found none who appealed to her and then bumped into me in the dining hall. I was not married and was polite and had a nice car. She decided that I would be an ideal partner and wanted a chance to show me that she was also ideal for me, but I kept hiding from her. I somehow had to convince her that I was happy with my own company and persuade her to broaden her search.

"Sue, I lost my wife three years ago and have now settled in at a smaller house with lots of friends near my home in Yorkshire. I am sorry to hear how things have not worked out for you, but unfortunately, you chose the wrong partner. I know you would be the wrong partner for me, because you are using the wrong reasons for choosing me. Choose someone who shares your interests and lives near you, so that you can get to know them and avoid making the same mistake again."

"I know we would get on together, because you are the sort of man I always wanted."

"Sue, you know nothing about me and I already have my own life in Yorkshire and don't need a partner. You will have to keep on looking but find someone who also wants to be your partner. Now, no more following me please."

I left her in the cafeteria and walked to my room, feeling sorry for her, but hoping that my words had convinced her that there was no chance of attracting me. I could not understand why she had stayed with her partner for so long in spite of his violence towards her and his continued laziness and gambling. Our last day was to be spent indoors at the university.

Next day, we were in the classroom where Jennie reviewed our paintings to discuss faults and solutions. In the afternoon, the marks for each of our paintings, as awarded by other holiday guests, were counted and prizes awarded. I was amazed to learn that my painting of Crathes Castle was awarded third prize, which would be presented at our final dinner in the evening. I got back to my room and began to think about driving off in the morning through heavy traffic. I decided to pack and leave immediately to drive through the night when the roads were quiet. I could stop for a meal half way and would certainly not want to display my Crathes Castle painting on my wall. At seven o'clock, I left to drive towards Edinburgh and continued my journey south. After three hours, I stopped for a toilet and food break on the motorway near Edinburgh, filled up my petrol tank and drove off again. I was rolling along at 90 miles an hour near Berwick on Tweed with no other traffic on the road when the area around me suddenly lit up. I recognised it as the flash on a speed camera as it clocked my speed. I slowed down and accepted that I would in due course receive a demand for payment, since I was twenty miles over the speed limit. I had started out carefully observing the local traffic restrictions, but with so far to go and with such quiet roads, it is difficult not to add a little speed to try to shorten the journey. By three o'clock, I was back at home and could not wait to jump into bed.

Chapter 15
New Companion

Although I had only been away for four nights, the two long drives had made it seem so much longer. I slept until nine o'clock, had breakfast, read my mail and spent Friday morning shopping and planning my weekend. After all the activity over the past week, with places to go and people to see, my quiet morning felt like an anti-climax. After walking to Helen's house to ask about her course, there was no reply, so taking advantage of the sunshine, I strolled along to see how our estate garden was doing. There were weeds growing amongst the beds and the lawn needed cutting, which told me that the FGC rota was not being followed. My next stop was at The Yorkshireman to check with Rod on who the guilty party was. Rod hailed me as the wanderer returned and said he was tired of telling people that I was off somewhere painting. I felt guilty as I realised that while I was in Aberdeen, I should have telephoned Helen and Dickie to tell them where I was. The lawn should have been cut by a man who had been taken to hospital suddenly with an appendix abscess. During my sudden holiday, no one had thought to nominate a substitute and since it was my fault, I told him I would cut the estate garden lawn. Dickie was in York again after returning to find I was away, although Helen had returned before she too had gone away again. Rod told me it had brought tears to his eyes to look at our empty table in his bar night after night. He rubbed his eye to make his claim more convincing.

"Oh Rod. It really is touching to know that I have been missed and I promise I will be at our table tonight and for days afterwards, but it looks as if I will be eating alone."

I cut the lawn and pulled up enough weeds to fill a plastic bag before leaving the garden looking neat and tidy again. My telephone call to Helen was diverted to her voice mail and left me no wiser as to where she was, or what she was doing. Next, I rang Dickie who answered and asked where I had been for the last week.

"Sorry, Dickie, it would take too long to give you the full story on the phone, so tell me where you are."

"I thought you were just off to Manchester to speak to a meeting, but you buggered off again. I decided to go back to York to stay with Trudy and asked Rod to tell me when you came out of hiding. I thought that Gloria must have caught up with you again."

"No, I think Gloria got the message and was so annoyed with me that she should leave me alone now. Then when I was in Scotland, I got hounded by a woman again, but this time I stopped it going too far."

"What is it with you and all these women who can't leave you alone? If we could bottle it and sell it, we would make a fortune."

He wanted to know what I had been doing in Scotland and again I told him it was a long story and asked when he was coming back to York. He told me he would be back on

Saturday, because he wanted to know what I had been up to and he had news for me. He promised to return in time to join me for dinner at The Yorkshireman. My house needed a good clean after all the time I had spent away and it was almost 7 pm before I finished my cleaning and went to order dinner from Rod.

In his position as our neighbourhood watch coordinator, he had obtained window stickers, which stated that the area was active in crime prevention. They were available for resident members to place in their windows, which he hoped would help to deter possible break-ins. Either we were lucky, or the guidance on securing doors and windows had helped to keep crime on our estate at a very low level, which made everyone happy. After finishing my meal, I sat at the bar and told Rod about my free and unexpected painting holiday in Scotland. I also mentioned the likely speeding fine and he thought I might get lucky.

"Many of these speed cameras are broken, or have no film, but they can still make drivers slow down. You might just get away with it."

There were quite a few of our FGC members in the bar and they had heard about my canal walk from Rod and wanted to know when the walking group would be formed. We were due to hold our next meeting soon and I promised it would be on the agenda. As the result of being involved in so many conversations, I had done little drinking and counted this as another benefit from a very productive evening with FGC members. I went home to recover after my lost sleep and long drive when returning from the Aberdeen course. Next morning a parcel arrived in the post from Jennie Hockeysticks. She had sent me my painting of Crathes Castle and apologised for drinking the bottle of wine awarded to me for my prize. After my sudden departure, she used my wine to toast my success and since it was opened and would not keep, she had finished it off with more toasts to my success. She also explained that she would have been unable to fit it into the envelope anyway. She was disappointed that I had not said goodbye and urged me to return next year as one of her advanced students. I suspected that if there was any advance activity, it was more likely to come from Jennie. It was time for another round of golf with our FGC sponsor, Arthur, and I rang him to arrange a 10 am drive off at the golf club.

Arthur was pleased with the publicity and kind comments about his sponsorship from residents and in the local newspaper. After driving his ball into the deep rough alongside the fairway, I went to help him in his search and accidentally trod on his ball. Holding it up and checking the number, it was very definitely one of his, but unfortunately, it lay behind a very large tree. His first recovery shot hit the tree and his ball bounced back to land beside me. Once again, I checked the number and Arthur then took four more shots before breaking out of the wood and landing in long grass alongside the fairway. Unfortunately, his ball was set deep in the grass and it took him two more strokes to get it to the middle of the fairway. I have never hit the ball with such accuracy and every stroke seemed to be drawn to the centre of the green. On the eighteenth hole, I sank the ball with an incredible twenty feet put and assured Arthur that it must have been my once-in-a-lifetime golden round. He bought the drinks as the loser and quoted some of my scores to fellow golfers, who seemed more amazed than impressed, having watched my usual standard of play.

I was relieved to watch Dickie coming to join me as I sat at our table for an evening meal in the pub. While we were eating, I told him about the Altrincham meeting and generous offer by Diane to take her painting holiday. I also produced my signed copy of my Crathes Castle masterpiece and told him I was reproducing it with a good-looking man at his easel in the foreground, plus twelve young Japanese girls admiring his work. It could well make me a serious rival to David Hockney, who often produced quirky paintings with mixed backgrounds. Dickie was not impressed, but as a potential advanced student, I felt sure that Jennie Hockeysticks would appreciate its merits. I could sense that Dickie was distracted and after clearing his throat, he gave me his news.

"Me and Trudy are getting married."

He was watching me closely and waiting to hear my response to his announcement, which I had been half expecting. I shook him by the hand.

"Congratulations. Trudy is just the woman you need to bring love and enjoyment into your life. So, when is the wedding?"

He told me the wedding would be in three months, so that he could put his own house up for sale and allow Trudy time to convince her daughter that he was the right man for her. Dickie then asked if I would be his best man.

"Thank you for asking me and yes, I would be happy to be your best man and see you finally start a new life with the right woman."

We were so engrossed in our conversation that we did not see Helen approaching with her drink in her hand.

"You two look like conspirators planning something evil with your heads down and close together."

We both greeted Helen as she sat down beside me. I told her that I had missed her as she was off on some mysterious courses and it was good to see her back again. Instead of telling us about her courses, Helen told me that when she came back a few days after leaving me asleep in her house, she was told that I had gone away and no one had any idea where I was. I apologised again for falling asleep after her superb lasagne and explained that I had slept badly the previous night and obviously drunk too much wine. Helen gave me a big smile and needed more answers.

"Was your problem with getting to sleep anything to do with someone called Gloria by any chance?"

Dickie and I both stared at each other in shock, before I turned to look directly at Helen.

"Yes, it was, Helen. I was very annoyed with Gloria, but even more so with myself because I had to charge across to Leeds to meet her and listen to all her marriage problems. That was before refusing to stay the night at the Queens Hotel, which is what she was demanding."

Helen nodded her head after hearing my explanation and told us how she had heard Gloria's name.

"After finishing washing up in the kitchen, I brought you coffee and found you were fast asleep, so I put a blanket around you. You were quite restless and muttered the name Gloria twice and it sounded as if you two were having an argument."

"We certainly had an argument. We were together on the Route 66 tour and she was a very lonely but very devious woman, and when we were in Las Vegas, I was tempted by her charms. She managed to make desire overcome my natural discretion. We were on holiday and as far as I was concerned, we both behaved unwisely and should have left it at that. Unfortunately, Gloria had other ideas and wanted to start an affair here, but I refused and left her a very angry woman. I knew that I should not have been tempted in America and accept that it was my fault, even though with hindsight, I know that she had chosen me as her holiday romance candidate."

To my relief, I noticed a slight relaxation in Helen's previous tense posture, probably due to me having ruined her dinner by falling asleep and then raving about Gloria. Now she knew the truth and could make her own judgement. As I waited to hear what Helen thought, Dickie rose to his feet and told us that he had things to do and had to leave us. Left to ourselves, I told Helen about Dickie getting married and that I was to be his best man. Helen asked me how I would manage without my long-term companion.

"I am hoping that we can spend more time together, since we have lots in common and in particular the ability to fall asleep to avoid drinking each other's coffee."

Helen laughed and nodded her head as she heard this.

"Touché. So how was the talk with the Altrincham group?"

I described the meeting and having to spend the night at Elaine's large house with the very active small dogs. Helen was surprised to hear that I had been addressing an all-female audience and her eyebrows rose when I mentioned spending the night at Elaine's house. I wanted to explain why it had been a genuine case of hospitality.

"Elaine is a widow and retired solicitor who is now very active in the local community and politics. She lives in a very large house on her own because she needs the garden for her two dogs. She agreed to provide me with accommodation only after Diane had told her I was trustworthy and invited both of us to stay if we ever want to visit the Tatton Park flower show."

"How does Elaine know anything about me?"

"When I was speaking to Diane and Elaine about setting up the FGC, I also told them how we worked closely together and that you were my friend and neighbour. They know I am keen on gardening, which is why they were offering us the option of staying with Elaine if we ever wanted to go to the Tatton Park flower show. Elaine would welcome our company and it would then be an easy drive to the show."

Again, I waited for a response, but instead Helen just changed the subject with a surprising invitation.

"It looks like it will be a nice day tomorrow. How about giving me a game of tennis?"

"I didn't know you could play tennis or I would have invited you to play long ago. Yes, I would like to play, but have you got a racquet?"

Helen nodded her head and assured me that she had a racquet. She then stood and told me she had been driving for hours to get back and it was time for bed. We left and to my surprise, on the way back to our houses, she took my arm and then waved goodnight as we reached her house. I felt disappointed that I had not at least been given a peck on the cheek for my honesty in answering her questions about Gloria but had long ago given up trying to understand ladies and their unpredictable behaviour.

We were on court together at 10 am and Helen looked very attractive in her neat skirt and top. I knocked the first ball over so that we could adjust to the ball bounce and warm up and was pleased to see Helen striking the ball well and keeping it over the net and on court. We had a good game and although Helen was not able to hit the ball hard, or use spin, she moved well around the court and returned most of the serves. After our game, we got changed and Helen invited me back to her house for coffee. She asked where I had gone after the meeting at Altrincham and I described receiving the free painting holiday from Diane and promised to show her my prize-winning painting of Crathes Castle. She was obviously still turning over in her mind my overnight stay with Elaine.

"How is it that you impressed Diane so much that she told Elaine you were to be trusted at her house?"

I explained that we were sitting together for hours on the flight back from Los Angeles after finishing the tour along Route 66 and Helen accused me of being able to charm the birds out of the trees with my silvery tongue. I defended myself by insisting that I liked people, was willing to listen as they talked about themselves or their problems and tried to cheer them up. Helen shook her head.

"As I see it, you generally seem to enjoy listening to ladies, who all like talking to you. I have watched you charm them and how they all come under your spell, even if you are not always aware of it. Come on, let me have a look at this masterpiece. I had no idea that you were a painter as well."

We went along to my house and I produced the painting and described how the Japanese students, all young girls of course, had stood behind to watch me painting. I also told her that there were superb gardens and a walk beside the lake and through the woods, which unfortunately there was no time for me to visit, but I hoped to return. When I told Helen that I was thinking of reproducing the painting, with me and the

Japanese girls in the foreground, she liked the idea. I felt we were beginning to get along together really well and hoped that I would not spoil things again. We spoke about the proposed walking club addition and I described my trial walk from Leeds Wharf to Salts Mill along the canal towpath. When I spoke about the danger from inconsiderate cyclists and my idea about wearing tabards, Helen though she could make one, but I would need to find a way to have the red wording added. It was a nice day and a good time to go back to Saltaire.

"How about joining me for a walk around the village of Saltaire near Salts Mill? When I was there last week, I was too tired to explore the village and riverbank. I can make us a quick snack first."

"You already told me you were a terrible cook, so just show me what you have in your larder and let me see what I can make."

Helen quickly made a snack from my well-stocked larder and we drove off to Saltaire. We spent the afternoon walking around the old stone-built village and church before crossing the river and taking a ride on the Cable Tramway up to Shipley Glen. Afterwards, we went on a boat trip along the Leeds and Liverpool Canal and I pointed out the towpath I had used for my trial walk. As we were walking back along the towpath to Salts Mill, a small brown dog began to follow us and when we stopped and sat on a wall; the dog also sat and was facing Helen. I recognised the breed.

"I think it must be a Border Terrier and it seems to be missing a collar."

Before I could stop her, Helen took a biscuit from her bag and gave it to the dog, who gulped it down and then sat on its haunches waiting for more. I knew that having fed the dog, we now had little hope of sending it away. Fortunately, instead of giving it more biscuit, Helen began stroking it and was rewarded by having her hand licked furiously.

"I have always wanted a dog. I wonder if it belongs to someone, but is lost or perhaps has strayed."

"All dog owners are now required by law to have a microchip implanted in the dog's neck and it must also have a collar. With no collar, this dog could be a stray, or perhaps has been abandoned."

"Would I be able to keep it if it is a stray?"

"Since we would now have a problem trying to send it away after you have fed it and it has obviously taken a liking and a licking for you, we could take it back in my car and get a vet to check the microchip. We must then return the dog to the owner, but if it is not microchipped and you want to keep it, you would need to get it chipped and buy a collar."

Helen hugged me and with the dog following close behind, we walked back to the car for the drive back. We seemed to be more relaxed in each other's company and I saw it as our first date, since we were together for pleasure instead of working on FGC activity. I left Helen and her dog at her house and we arranged to meet later that evening. We met up with Dickie at our local pub and he confirmed that his house was up for sale and that he had started making his arrangements to move to York for his new start with Trudy.

"We will all miss you, Dickie, but it is only a short drive in both directions for us to keep in touch. Are you thinking of teaching Trudy to shoot so that she can come with us to shoot clays occasionally?"

Dickie had no idea if Trudy would be interested in shooting, but he knew that she liked walking and they had driven to the North York Moors twice already. We enjoyed our evening together and as we were walking back to our houses, I told Helen that I felt sad that after so many years, there might not be so many more like it. Helen took my arm and shook it.

"Cheer up, you lead such a busy life that you are always making new friends and getting involved in new activities. If you promise not to fall asleep again, you can come to dinner tomorrow night after we prepare for the next meeting and discuss how you think the walking group should be run. Would you like to take me and the dog to the vet first?"

"Thank you, Helen, and yes, I would be happy to take you and Bonzo to the vet and I would also like to come to dinner. I am sorry to be such a grouch, but Dickie and I have been close friends for a very long time. I promise I will do my best not to fall asleep again."

"I will just have to do my best to make sure that you don't, won't I? And if I do get to keep the dog, he will certainly not be called Bonzo."

First thing the following morning, Helen and her dog were at my front door and we went to the local vet, who could find no trace of a microchip. Helen could not believe her luck in finding she could now keep Bonzo, which I insisted was better than calling him "dog". A microchip was fitted and we called at a store to get the dog a collar with Helen's name and telephone number inscribed. Back at her house, we had lunch and choose a name for her new lodger. I suggested "Billy", which was short and easy to remember, and to my surprise, Helen agreed.

In the evening, I arrived at Helen's door at 6 pm as requested and held a large bunch of red roses, which the florist assured me would be well received by any lady. Helen appeared at the door in a red dress with an apron covering the front and I could not help noticing her low-cut top and tight skirt, which emphasised her woman appeal to me. Since I had mostly seen her in jeans and anoraks, her appearance came as quite a surprise. She took me to her lounge to see some of her photographs while she was finishing her preparations. There were views of Helen on a tennis court with a healthy-looking young man in tennis shorts and some of her on a golf course with a slightly older man beside a golf trolley with a well-filled golf bag. I had just finished working my way through the photographs when Helen asked me to sit down at her dining table. Once again, there was wine on the table, but this time it was white wine in an ice bucket and I guessed we were having fish. After melon with palma ham to start, we had monkfish with pilau rice and a mix of chopped vegetables. Monkfish has a dense, almost meaty texture and is not often on sale in supermarkets.

"I can't remember the last time I had monkfish, Helen, where did you find it?"

"There are really good fishmongers in the central market and I shop there when I want something special."

"And tonight is special, is it?"

"It might be, if you want to make it so."

Billy was sleeping in his new basket and seemed to have already settled in his new home. After we finished eating, I insisted on standing beside Helen to help with washing up and was given an apron to protect my best trousers. We took our coffee into the lounge and sat down together on a settee as I pointed to the photographs and asked where Helen had been. I was surprised to hear that she had been on both a tennis training course in Eastbourne, as well as a golf course at The Belfry near Sutton Coldfield. I was impressed that she had been so determined to learn the basics of both games but puzzled by her decision to learn both games so suddenly.

"Why were you in such a hurry to learn tennis and golf, Helen?"

Ignoring my question, Helen asked if I would like a Drambuie after my coffee and when we both had small glasses in our hands, she gave me her explanation.

"When we made love, I was shocked and embarrassed by my behaviour and then I had another shock when I found that my long-time friend no longer wanted to see me. You were very sympathetic and I was surprised by just how much I enjoyed being with you. When I met Jean, I could see that she was very special to you, but you never seemed to appreciate this. I really liked her and was upset when she told me in confidence that she was fighting cancer. She described her symptoms and knew from my facial expression that it was very serious and asked me to promise that after she had gone, I would look after you. You were badly affected by Jean's death and because she had kept her illness such a secret. Dickie and I were both worried about you because you seemed to have lost your usual vital spark. We thought a holiday would help and Dickie persuaded you to go with him along Route 66. I am not sure whether it was the holiday or Gloria who charged you up again, but we were pleased that the holiday had worked."

"Thank you, Helen. You and Dickie have been such incredible friends to me and with Dickie moving away soon,

I am hoping we can see more of each other, particularly since you now play tennis and golf. Although I am still surprised that you were in such a hurry to have lessons."

Helen smiled at me and took my hand but gave no reason for her sudden urge to learn both games and instead spoke of our relationship.

"I enjoy your company Tom, but you do seem to gather lady friends wherever you go and I know that will never change. We work together on FGC affairs and we are neighbours and if we also play tennis and golf together, perhaps I will be with you often enough to protect you from other ladies like Gloria."

I was startled to hear how much effort Helen had put into honouring her promise to Jean but was more encouraged by her admission that she enjoyed being with me. Although I had never been able to understand, or predict female behaviour, my intuition was screaming at me that here was a lovely woman and I enjoyed being with her too. I put down my glass and reached out to take Helen's before moving closer and putting my arms around her. Helen tilted her head and we kissed and as we snuggled up close together, I breathed a message in her ear:

"We are both awake and if we choose to go to bed now, it will not be on impulse, or a dream, but because we want to."

Helen stood up and took my hand before leading me to her bedroom. We made love and Helen told me that I was just as enthusiastic when I was awake as when I was dreaming. I assured her that it had never been the dream but had always been the woman who raised my enthusiasm. We fell asleep with our arms wrapped around each other. I was still sleeping in the morning when I was poked in the ribs and woke up wondering who was assaulting me.

"So tell me more about this Gloria who was with you on Route 66."

I described meeting the two ladies from Croydon and how Gloria was becoming increasingly amorous as we moved along our way west. I began to anticipate the inevitable next question.

"And how exactly did Gloria manage to get desire to overcome your natural discretion?"

"Dickie and I were in a restaurant and were joined by the two ladies and Gloria sat beside me and Dorothy beside Dickie. The lights were dimmed for the cabaret and Gloria took hold of my hand and then pressed it between her legs."

"Was she wearing underwear?"

"Almost, but it was mainly space and lace."

"Mine tonight were mainly space and lace."

"You have no need to wear space and lace if you want to encourage me. Just being near me is enough."

Helen laughed and put her arms around me and we delayed getting out of bed. After breakfast, I returned home after a very long kiss from Helen. I telephoned Dickie and asked him if we could meet up for a coffee and a chat, but instead, he suggested lunch because he was busy with an estate agent. In my post was a letter from the Scottish police demanding payment for my speeding fine. Obviously, the camera I drove past did have film in it. If it was a case of lucky in love and unlucky with speed cameras, I was happy to accept that. When I met Dickie, he was very pleased with the price he could get when his house was sold. He bought it twenty-five years ago and prices since then have soared, but although his house value has increased, so too have the prices of any property he might want to buy. If Trudy wanted to carry on living in the bungalow left to her by her friend Jean, then his property money would be a useful bonus for both of them. I thanked him for his help in taking me on holiday after Jean died and he asked about my relations with Helen.

"How are you and Helen getting along now that she knows all about Gloria?"

I told him that we were now closer than ever and described how she had taken training courses both for tennis and golf just so that we could spend more time with each other.

"She must really think a lot of you to go to all the trouble and expense of going on those courses just to help you."

"You're right and I know I would have found it very difficult to set up the FGC without her help."

Dickie put his arm on my shoulder and offered me some advice.

"You have reorganised your life and I know you are enjoying being on your own, but you regret not having told Jean how you felt about her and now you could be making the same mistake with Helen. Just think about it."

As I walked home, I thought again about how Helen had always been willing to help with the FGC and regularly sat with Dickie and me at our evenings in The Yorkshireman. She had taken courses on tennis and golf just to spend more time with me after Jean died and because Dickie would be spending most of his time with Trudy. I felt guilty that just as I had taken Jean for granted, I could now be doing exactly the same with Helen, just to maintain my lifestyle as a senior single. It dawned on me that Helen was very special to me and

I really did want to become part of a loving couple again and Helen would be my ideal companion.

I had just got back home when my phone rang and Helen wanted to know whether we should take advantage of the sunny afternoon and have another game of tennis. I told her it was a good idea and would pick her up in my car. It would give me an opportunity to tell her about my feelings as well as having an enjoyable afternoon together. We had a good game and as we were walking off the court, Helen asked me if we could go straight back home to get changed instead of changing in the clubhouse. As I was parking the car, Helen asked me to wait in her lounge and ten minutes later, she came back with coffee and I was surprised to see her still in her tennis skirt and top. We drank our coffee and as we sat near each other on her settee, I suspected that she had taken off her bra. Seeing me staring at the rounded shapes inside her top, Helen smiled and leaned forward to kiss me. When I took her in my arms, I found she had removed her bra and the rest of her underwear as well and my desire surged. We made passionate love on her settee and I could not believe this was the same woman who had hurried from my bed the morning after working together on the estate garden. Releasing her to get changed, I was in her kitchen washing up the coffee cups when she came up behind me and put her arms around me before whispering in my ear:

"Somehow, I don't think you had any problems choosing desire in place of discretion."

"No, and I know that I never shall with you and thank you for a wonderful afternoon. I was listening to Dickie over lunch as he told me how happy he was about meeting the right woman and suddenly I knew that I had met mine. Will you marry me, Helen?"

Helen moved back, folded her arms and stood watching me for what seemed like an age before putting her arms around me and giving me her answer.

"I thought you would never ask and decided it was time to give you just a little nudge. Of course I will marry you and if you buy me a shotgun as a wedding present, you can teach me to shoot and we can go together to your shooting club now that Dickie will not be joining you very often."

"We will make it a perfect wedding, Helen, and this afternoon, I am taking you to Leeds to choose an engagement ring so that everyone will know you are now a promised woman."

"I like that much better than being a fallen woman after you attacked me in your bed and claimed you were dreaming."

"I don't know who took advantage of the other that night, Helen, but whoever it was, it brought us together and that is all that really matters."

After giving me a quick kiss on the cheek, Helen said she wanted to make me a special meal to celebrate our engagement, but I insisted instead that after choosing the ring, we should stay in Leeds to enjoy a special engagement dinner.

"We will find a really good restaurant and ask for a corner table so that you can sit and admire your engagement ring and I will be happy to just sit there and admire my new fiancée."

Putting her arms on my shoulders and looking directly into my eyes, Helen paid me a compliment but also added a caution and a request.

"I feel so happy too and know you will make a wonderful husband, just as long as I am with you to fend off all your friendly ladies. Would you be happy for us to have a one-year engagement so that I know you can resist these ladies and it will also give us plenty of time to plan and prepare for our life together?"

Thinking about my amorous encounters over the past year I knew there would be challenges, but I was sure I could prove to Helen that I was ready and able to settle down. I gave her my word that during our engagement, I would resist all temptations.

Now that is another story.